THE
RAMBLE HOUSE
MAPBACKS

THE
RAMBLE HOUSE
MAPBACKS

by

Gavin L. O'Keefe

RAMBLE HOUSE

2013

The RAMBLE HOUSE Mapbacks

Gavin L. O'Keefe

If there was ever an author whose novels *should* have been published as Dell 'mapbacks,' it was Harry Stephen Keeler. One can easily imagine his unique mystery novels sitting alongside such original mapback titles as *The Affair of the Scarlet Crab* by Clifford Knight (Dell #75, 1945), *Murder Wears Mukluks* by Eunice Mays Boyd (Dell #259, 1948) and *The Case of the Seven Sneezes* by Anthony Boucher (Dell # 334, 1949).[1] The editors at Dell, however, never appreciated the magic and charm of Keeler's books, and his novels never made it to mapback status during that period. In fact, Harry Stephen Keeler never achieved any paperback release in his own country during his lifetime.[2]

The Dell mapbacks began with *The Four Frightened Women* by George Harmon Coxe in 1943, and initiated a truly innovative cover design format in mass-market paperback fiction. With their bold, air-brushed-style front covers, and original back covers featuring maps of the localities featuring in the book, the books went on to number more than 600, and gained a popularity which endures, with collectors, to this day. Between 1943 and 1951, almost all Dell paperbacks featured an original mapback, the detailed designs mostly being executed by artist Ruth Belew. Many of these books were in the mystery genre, though the list also included westerns, adventure, romance and historical novels. Front cover artists included Gerald Gregg, Victor Kalin, George Fredericksen and Jerry Cummings.

For those who admire the wonderful style of the Dell mapback as well as the works of Harry Stephen Keeler, and who might have

---

1. References from *The Mighty Calhoon List O' Dell Paperbacks*, edited by Fender Tucker (Ramble House, 2003), and *The Book of Paperbacks* by Piet Schreuders (Virgin Books, 1981).

2. The only paperback editions of Keeler's books to appear, prior to Ramble House, were several cheap reprints issued by his main British publisher, Ward, Lock & Co.

fantasized about the two having once met, speculation has now turned to reality with the advent of that other innovative publisher of distinctive paperbacks, Ramble House of Vancleave, Mississippi. From the creative minds and hands of Fender Tucker and Jim Weiler, Ramble House was already proving itself to be an innovative publisher of the kind of 'pulp' and mystery fiction which had been so central to the Dell mapback series. It seemed a logical step to adopt the guise of the esteemed mapback design for a number of Harry Stephen Keeler's Ramble House books. This easily 'killed two birds with one stone': to finally allow the beautiful mapback format to clothe a Keeler book, and to pay homage to the innovation of the Dell paperback.

Having already been an admirer of Ruth Belew's back cover map designs, I was enthusiastic about devising mapback-style covers for some of the Ramble House Keeler titles. To date I have completed fourteen separate mapback Keelers, and there is scope to increase this number. We have focused primarily on Keeler books featuring a definite locale which lends itself to being portrayed as a map. Where a particular Keeler novel moved around from city to city, or from country to country, with no special central scene of murder or mayhem, we have chosen to respectfully decline a mapback cover.

For several of these Ramble House Keeler books I have assumed full Dell mapback regalia: not just the map on the back cover, but spine lettering in the Dell style, front cover with Dell-style dramatic design, and a specially designed Ramble House 'keyhole' motif directly based on the keyhole symbols used by Dell to denote their mapback and genre paperbacks. I have also made a point of reining in the colors used on these covers: the original Dell covers had minimal color ranges, especially evident on the back covers.

This limited palette, rather than restricting the impact of these covers, actually enhances the effect. With many of the slick mass-market paperback covers of today there is a confusing abundance of color: the advent of cheap color-reproduction has opened the sluice-gates to Technicolor. In the past days of war-time production restrictions, spot-color, and cheaper paper, the artists and designers of the day were working to produce the most eye-catching book designs to woo the eye and open the wallet of the potential book-buyer. With the blossoming of the paperback book in the United States there grew competition amongst publishing firms such as Dell, Penguin, Pyramid, Pocket, Avon, Ballantine, Bantam, and others, to dominate the market, and the work of the book designers and illustrators of the day was very much to the fore of the marketing push.

In retrospect, we now appreciate these books for their artistry and style, and gratefully acknowledge the lasting influence of the artists who created the covers. But especially Dell! Because Dell made mapbacks, and they were unique books. And it's a gesture of love to the mapback and to Harry Stephen Keeler and other authors that Ramble House is bringing back a little bit of the old magic.

THE
RAMBLE HOUSE
MAPBACKS

The Big River trilogy

The 'Big River' trilogy comprises the books *The Portrait of Jirjohn Cobb*, *Cleopatra's Tears* and *The Bottle with the Green Wax Seal*, and devising different maps for each book enabled me to amplify the 'micro' to the 'macro.' Most of the central activity and discussion takes place on Bleeker's Island in Big River. A flood is imminent, the waters are rising, there is a murderer amongst the group, and it's very much a race for time for the island's 'captives' to escape the island.

The map for *The Portrait of Jirjohn Cobb* shows the island and its several features. Though sparsely furnished, the details of the island are very important to the men trapped there who must explore every possibility in order to find a means of escape. I drew this map in black pen and digitally colored and enhanced it as I have done with the bulk of these works.

The map for *Cleopatra's Tears* zooms out to a large view of the whole Big River basin running through Shelby County. Inspired by the simple process-type coloring of the original mapbacks, I scanned an old WWII ordnance map (ironically, found on the verso of a Second World War-time book dust-jacket: war-time restrictions meant that old army maps were sometimes recycled as book jackets!) and digitally altered it to form a map of the Big River district. Serendipitously, this proved easier than expected, and Big River formed quite easily out of a map of some middle-eastern country!

The map for the final book in the Big River saga, *The Bottle with the Green Wax Seal*, combines the maps from the previous two books, putting the detailed island (which has altered slightly since the first book) into some perspective with its geographic location.

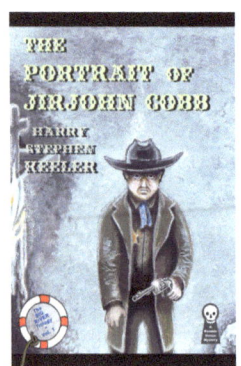  

The Portrait of Jirjohn Cobb
(1939)

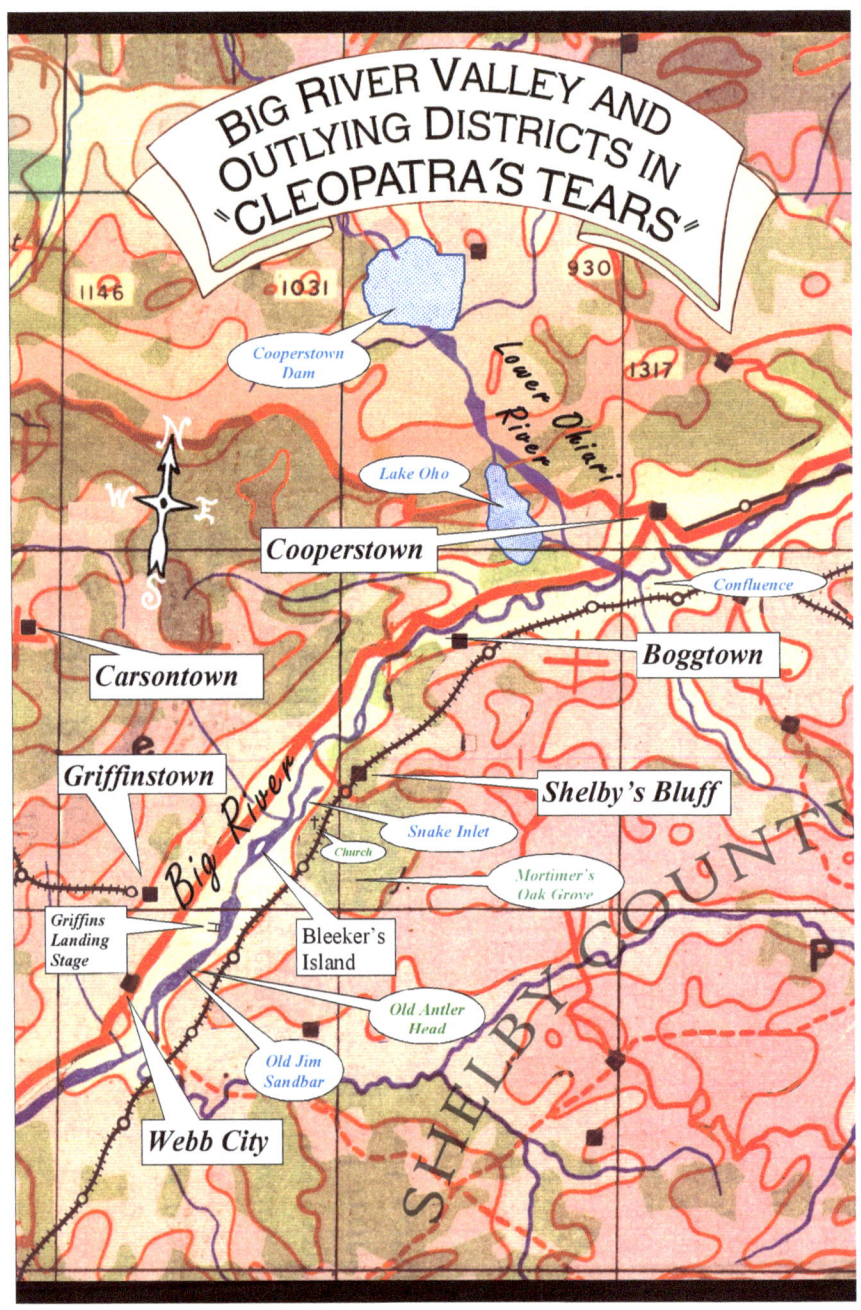

Cleopatra's Tears
(1940)

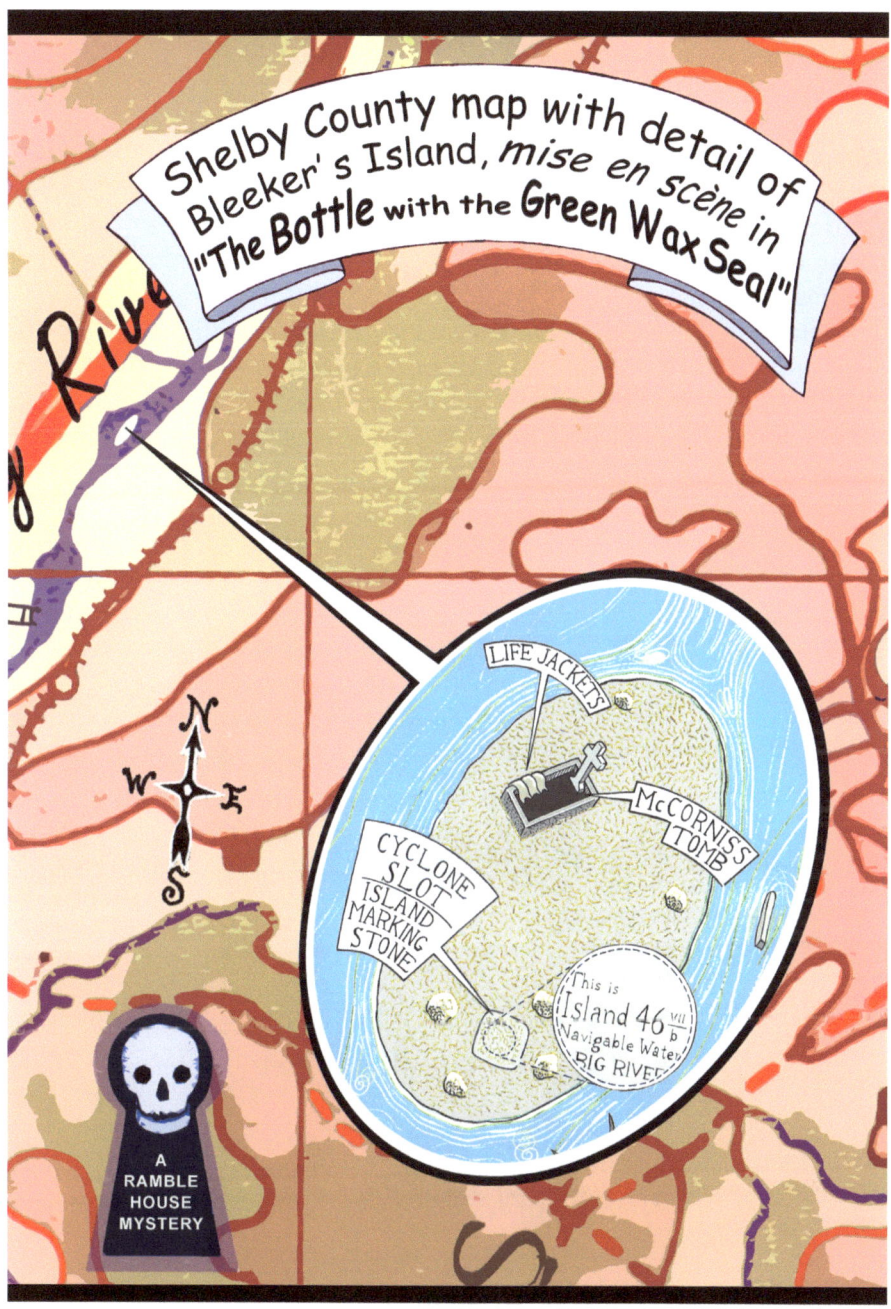

The Bottle with the Green Wax Seal
(1942)

The Mysterious Card

Whilst working on this map I was influenced by the original mapback design for *Gold Comes in Bricks* by A. A. Fair *aka* Erle Stanley Gardner (Dell #84, 1945), and I was inspired to keep to a similar color scheme and perspective. As before, I drew this map in black pen and digitally colored it.

Keeler's description of Harker's Crib, a one-room house, is quite clear and logical in the text, and I found it reasonably easy to create a plan for this murder scene.

This novel was published here for the first time, making it a mapback first edition.

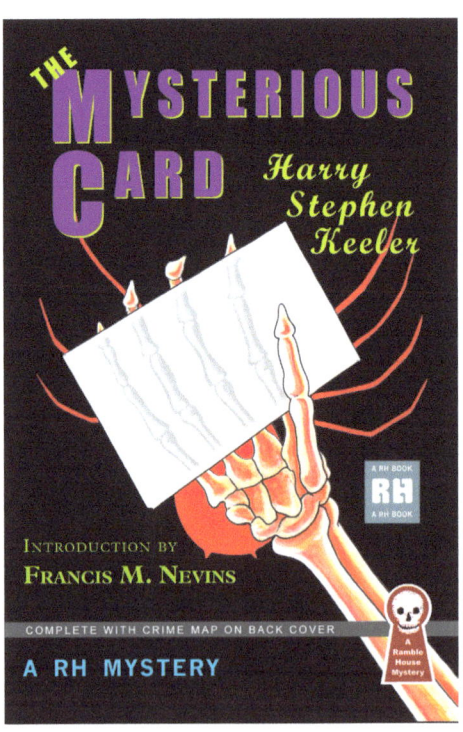

The Mysterious Card (2003)

The Case of the Flying Hands

This book includes three short stories: the title story written by Keeler's first wife Hazel Goodwin Keeler, and 'The Case of the Black Marbles' and 'The Case of the Hidden Munitions Spy' by Harry Stephen Keeler.

The map for this book depicts the two main sites where pivotal action occurs in Hazel's story 'The Case of the Flying Hands.' As I wanted to include both scenes, I ambitiously divided the frame diagonally into two, somewhat in the vein of the old television device of splitting the screen to show events or people, in two separate geographic locations, in real time.

In creating mapback designs based on Harry Stephen Keeler's books, I have gained the distinct impression that he himself planned his novel locales quite carefully. I wouldn't be surprised to learn that he actually drew rough maps as references for some of his books where convoluted journeys occur or where certain main streets or buildings are repeatedly referred to. In making this map for Hazel's story, however, I found it a challenge to translate the sometimes vague textual references to houses and streets into a concrete map.

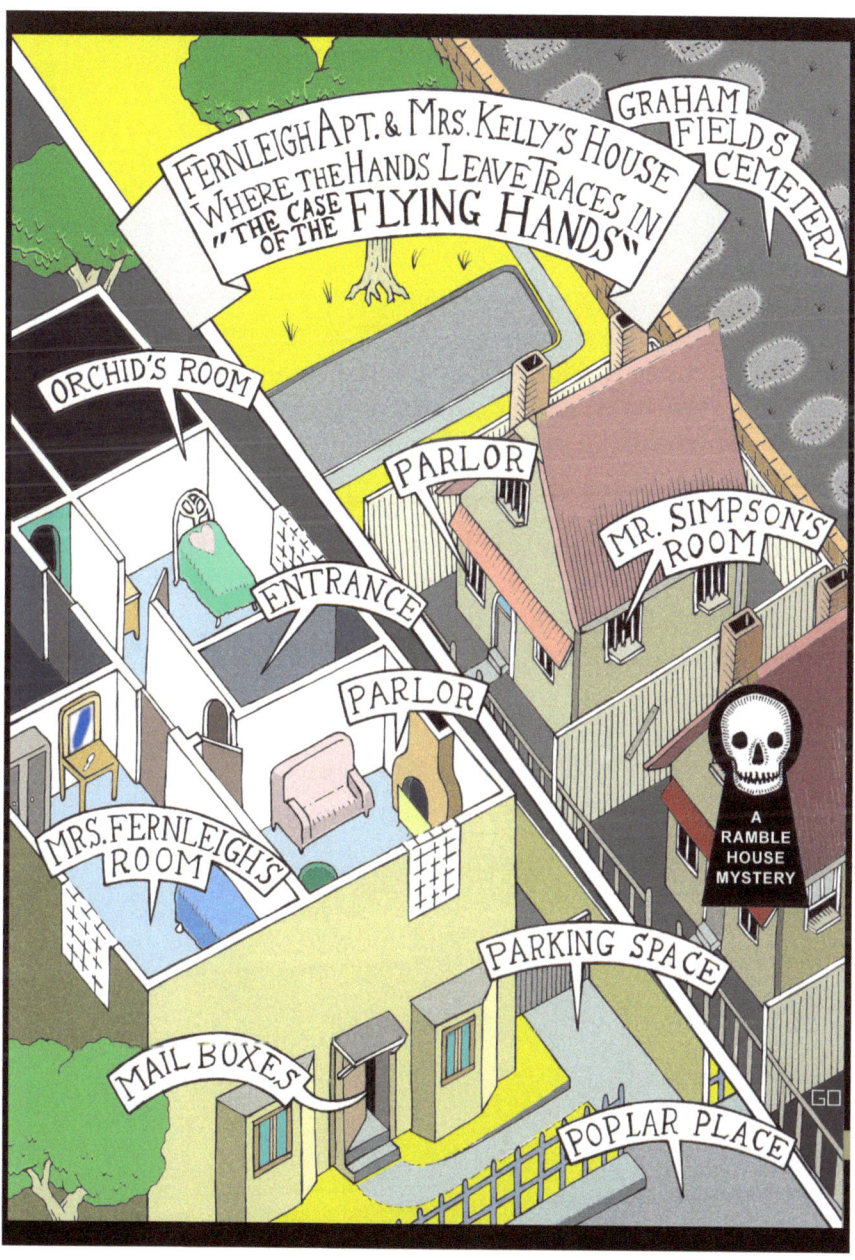

The Case of the Flying Hands
(2002)

The Photo of Lady X

This map represents the main district of 'Central City,' Keeler's alternate-reality version of Chicago. So, despite some street names being reminiscent of certain Chicago thoroughfares, this is a different, 'created' city.

The theme of chess runs throughout this novel in respect to the main characters or suspects. So, as well as creating a map of Central City which echoes actual Chicago, I further abstracted the map to conform to a strict chessboard pattern of streets. This was a contrived move on my part, but it matched the surreal front cover design (again incorporating a chessboard).

I was able to fit Keeler's street and building descriptions to my chessboard with some effort. Hazel Goodwin Keeler contributed a lengthy section to the book which involved additional streets and buildings, all which I was able to mesh with the main map.

This novel was published here for the first time, making it a mapback first edition.

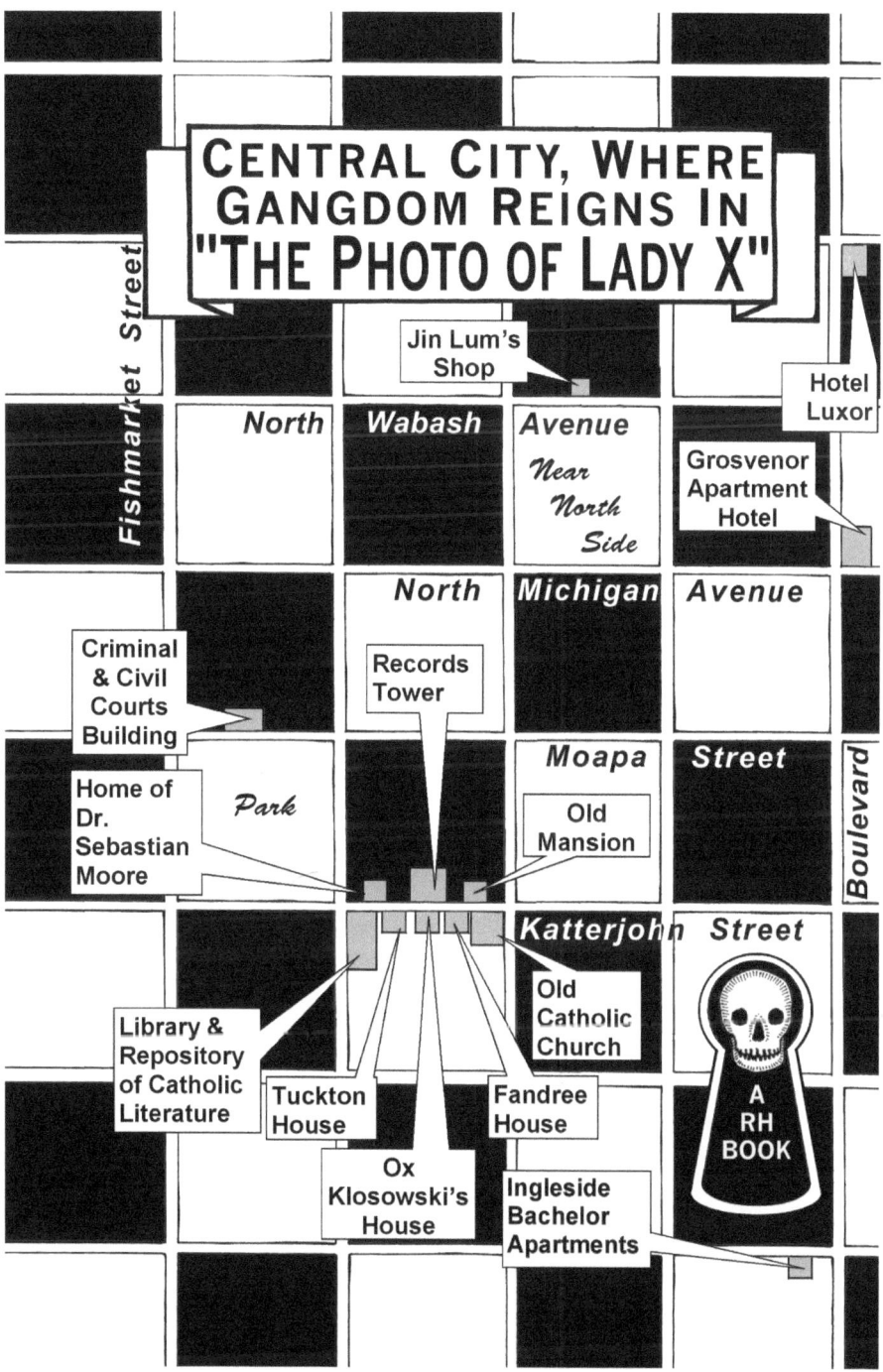

The Photo of Lady X (2003)

The Scarlet Mummy

This mapback design appears on one of Keeler's last novels, written with his second wife Tertza Rinaldo Keeler.

The events in this large novel take place in modern Chicago and ancient Egypt, with shifts in time from the mid-20th Century to 1720 B.C. As the ancient Egyptian theme (specifically, a mummy) appears throughout the book, I decided it would be nice to have a map of ancient Egypt showing the relevant main sites of action.

As a character travels between such far-flung cities as Thebes and Memphis, it was necessary to design a virtually complete map of ancient Egypt, thus representing a vast geographic area. I tried to keep things simple however by only indicating the sites described in the book. I also incorporated ancient Egyptian god motifs into the map and depicted the title banner as an ancient papyrus to give a flavor of the Egypt of yore.

This novel was published here for the first time, making it a mapback first edition.

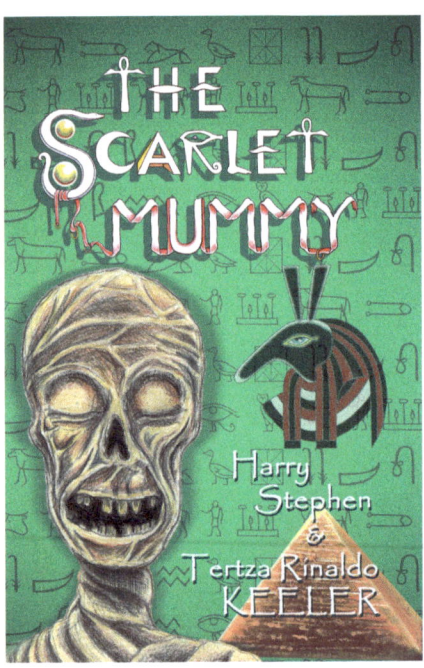

The Scarlet Mummy (2003)

The Search for X-Y-Z

This map portrays 'Wiscon City,' apparently another of Keeler's alternate-cities, this time reminiscent of Milwaukee.[1] However, I made no reference to maps of Milwaukee, and solely used the numerous descriptions in the text to construct the map.

I worked up the map in black ink and colored it digitally as with most of my maps.

Many of the Keeler books I've designed mapbacks for had descriptions of buildings or streets in only several, easily located places in the text. With *The Search for X-Y-Z*, however, I made sketches and notes as I read the book from start to end, as the details which helped to form my map were sprinkled throughout the whole book.

I had come across a book by James Hadley Chase, *Lay Her Among the Lilies* (Robert Hale, 1951), which reminded me of the need I had in this case to have a much larger map to refer to all the main sites in the novel. As opposed to the mapback format (ie., one single panel), this book has its map covering both of its endpapers:

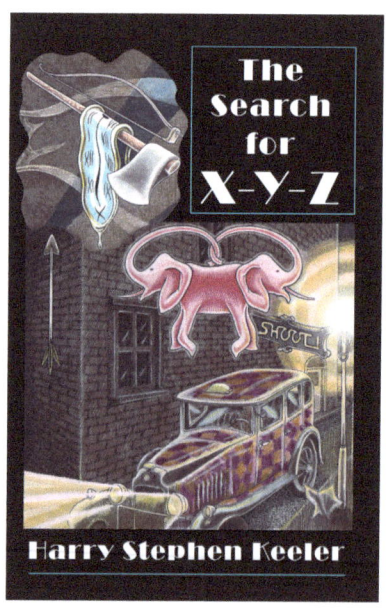

---

1. *Adventure in Milwaukee*, an earlier 'novello' from which Keeler may have elaborated parts of this novel, is actually set in Milwaukee.

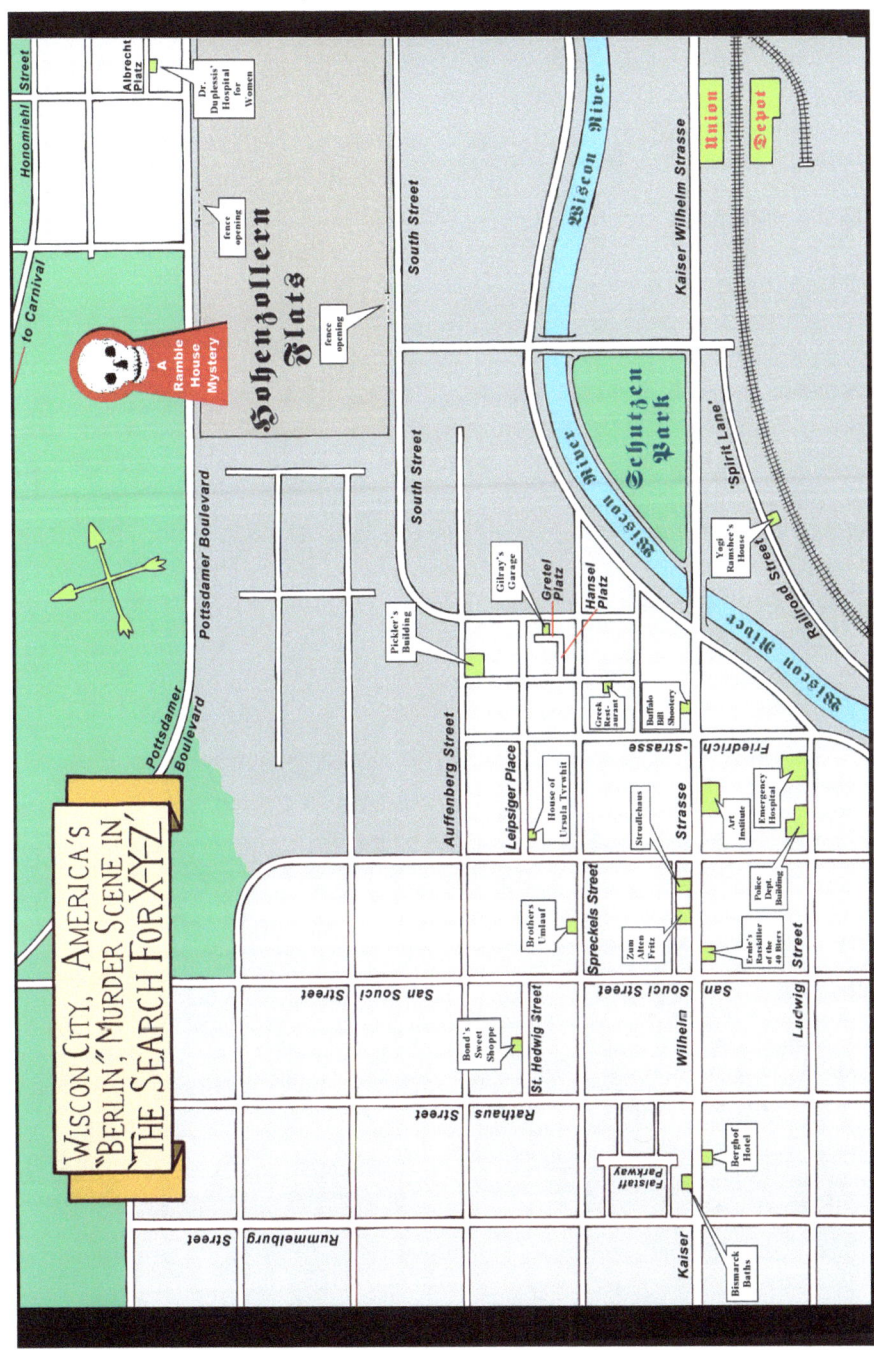

The Search for X-Y-Z (1943)

The Marceau Case
&
X. Jones – of Scotland Yard

The two maps on *The Marceau Case* and *X. Jones – of Scotland Yard* were based on the original diagrams by Jon Janecek which appeared in these 'dossier novels.'

The first map depicts the croquet lawn where the murder of André Marceau takes place, while the second presents a close-up of the murder scene with the supposed paths of the murderer and the victim. I redrew these diagrams in black ink, adding the trademark Dell mapback title banners and keyholes. I then added color and textures to some of the elements in the maps, and in the second map color-coded the character paths, which I 'explained' with a legend. Therefore, as opposed to my other Keeler maps, the presence of existing diagrams in the books themselves made my task very straightforward.

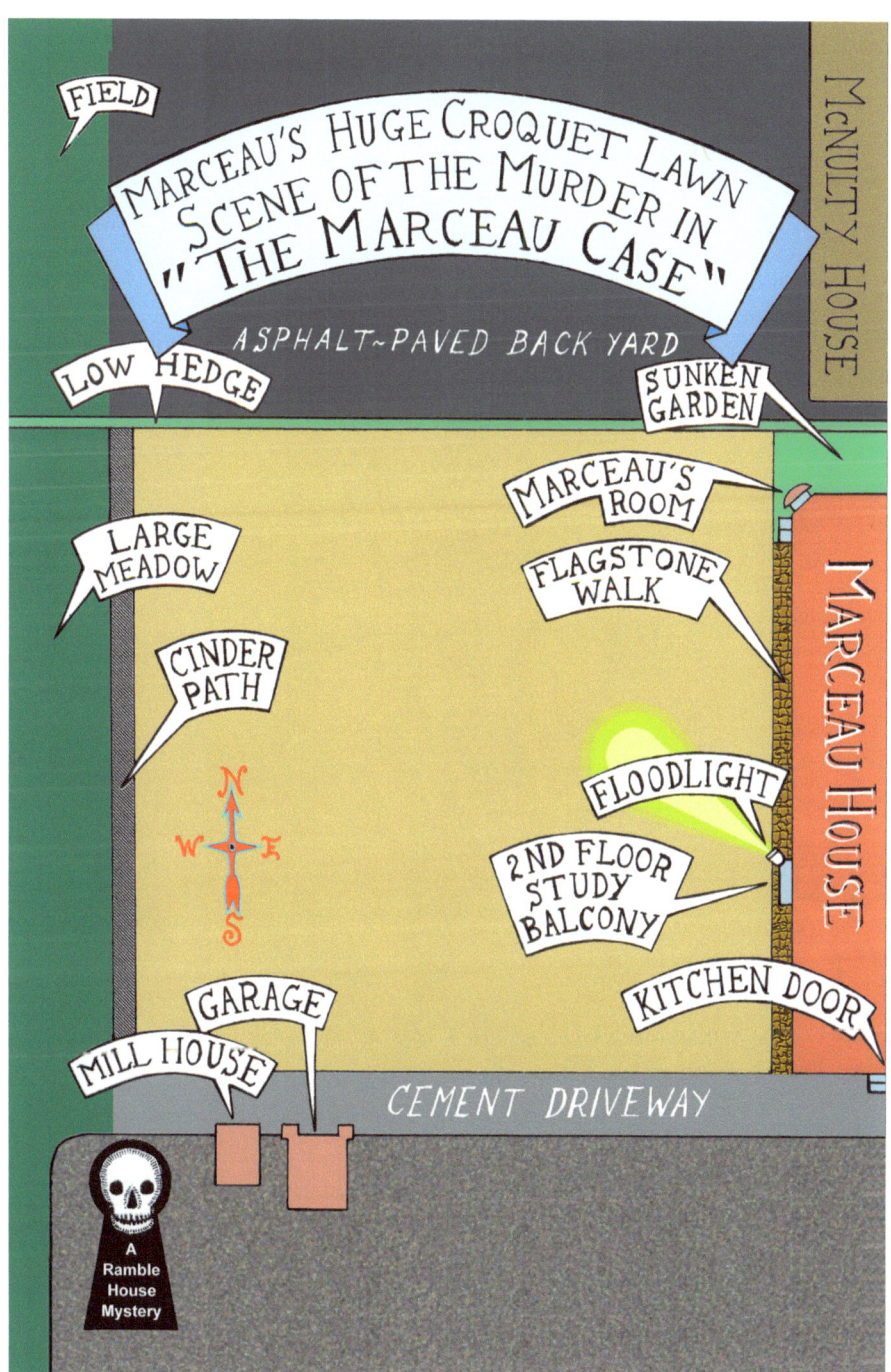

The Marceau Case (1936)

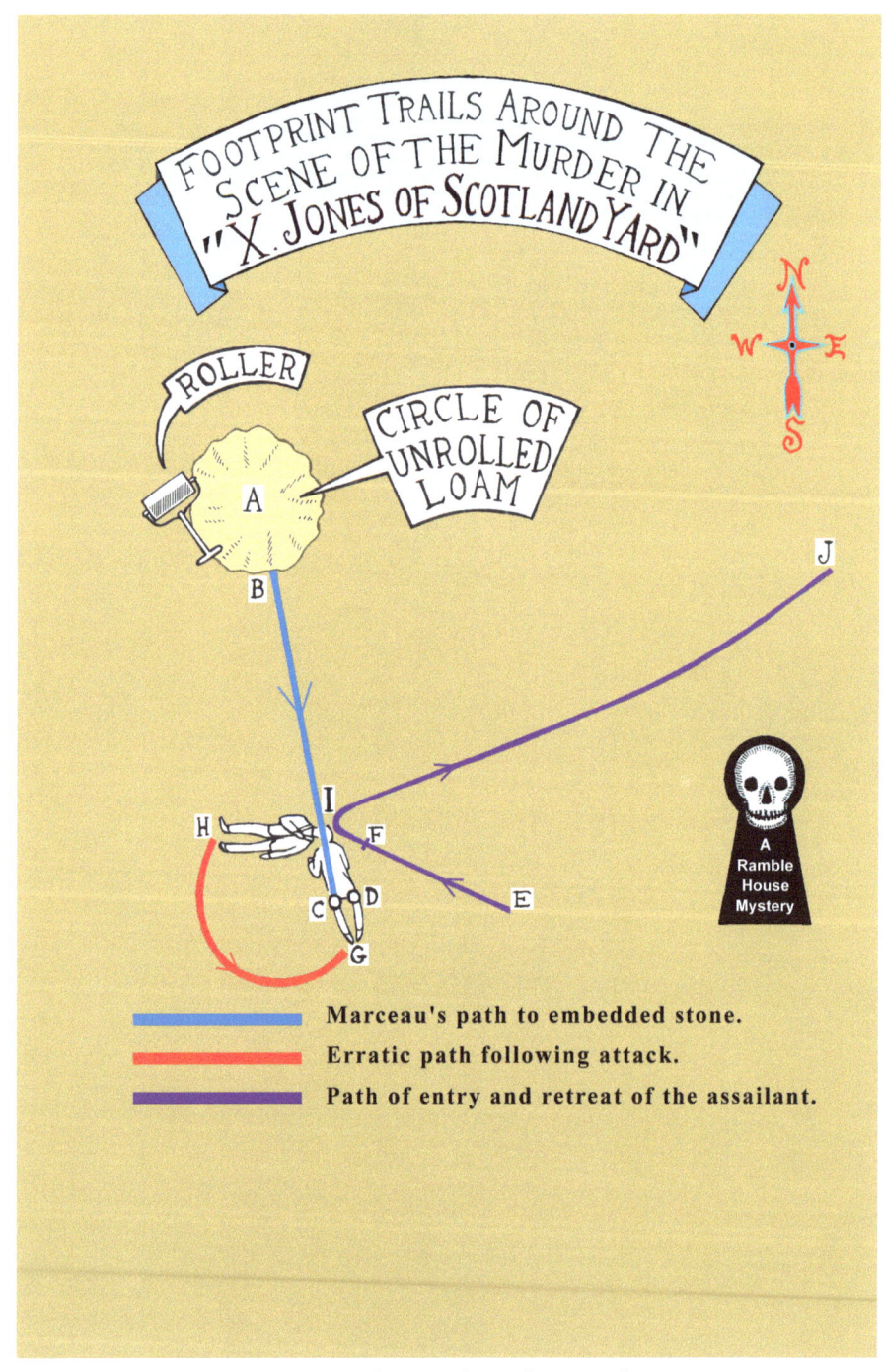

X. Jones—of Scotland Yard (1936)

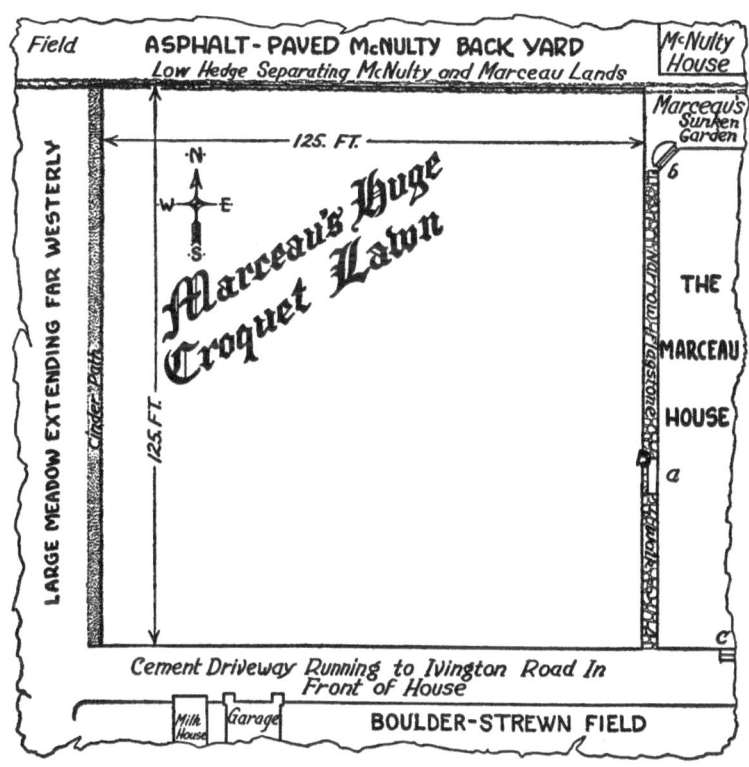

*Map of Marceau Croquet Lawn
taken from The Marceau Case*

The Steeltown Trilogy

The Case of the Canny Killer (Phoenix Press, 1946), *The Steeltown Strangler* (Ward Lock, 1950) and *The Crimson Cube* (written in 1954, and originally published in Spanish in 1960 by Instituto Editorial Reus of Madrid), comprise Keeler's 'Steeltown' trilogy set in the Tippingdale Steel Mills. Having himself once worked in a steel mill, Keeler rose to a challenge once set forth that it was impossible to write a novel set within a steel mill. With typical impish aplomb, Keeler even introduces within the plots of the books a young and successful novelist visiting Tippingdale in order to pick up details of steel mill 'color' and technical details to inform *his* proposed novel involving a steel mill!

The consistent layout of the site described in all three novels supports the suspicion that Keeler had a carefully worked-out plan of this steel mill complex handy for reference whilst writing the books. It is quite probable that the Tippingdale Steel Mills ("one square mile in extent, with 85 sep'rate mill buildings") is based on Keeler's memory of the steel factory where he once worked.

My mapback design of the mills valiantly attempts to delineate the complexity of this sprawling industrial site.

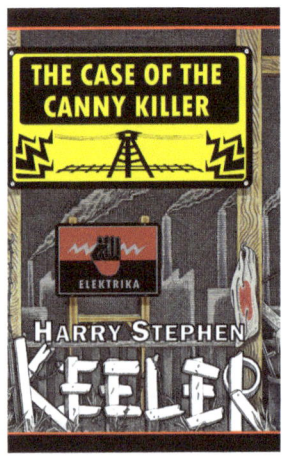  

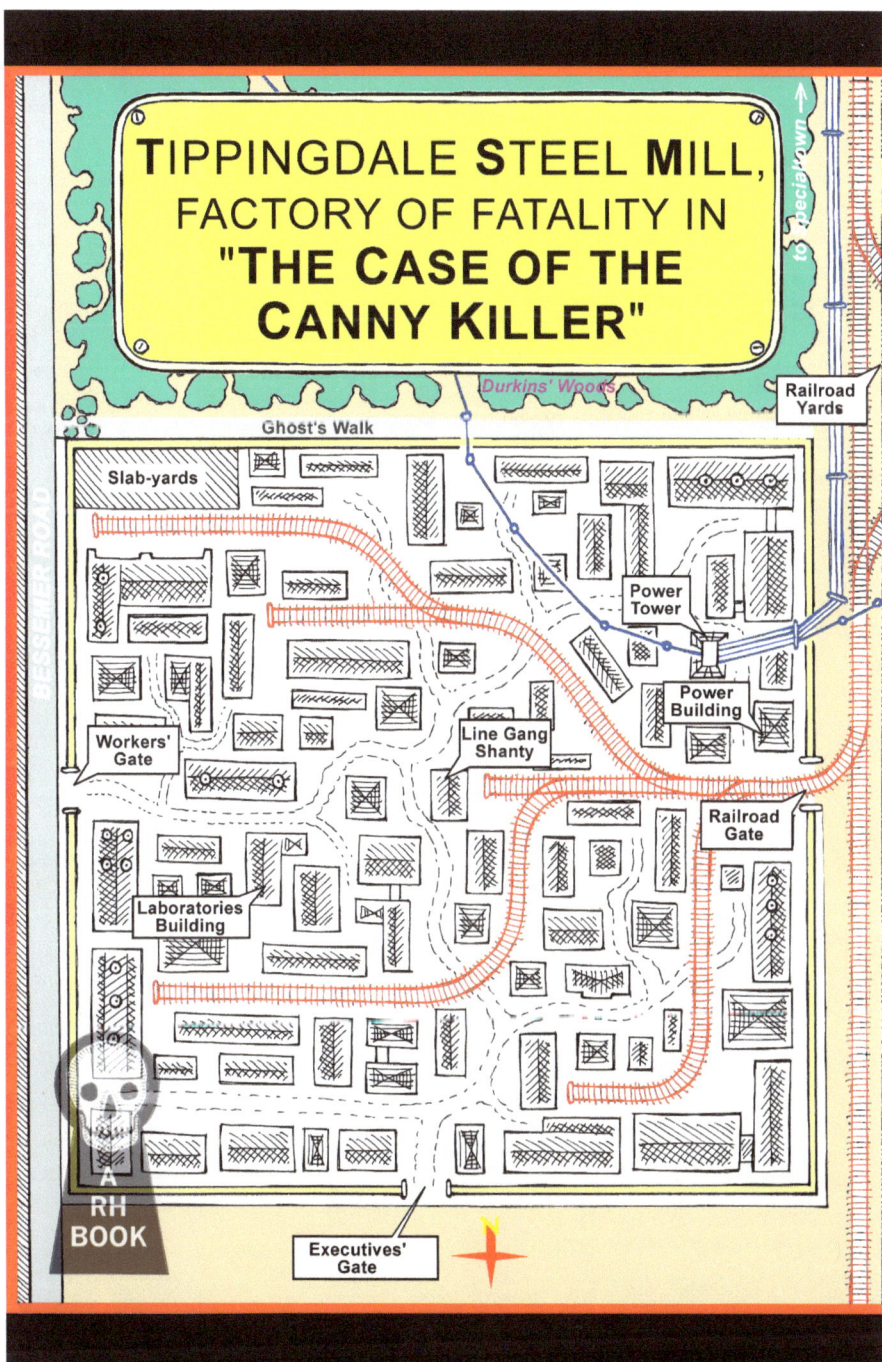

The Case of the Canny Killer (1946)

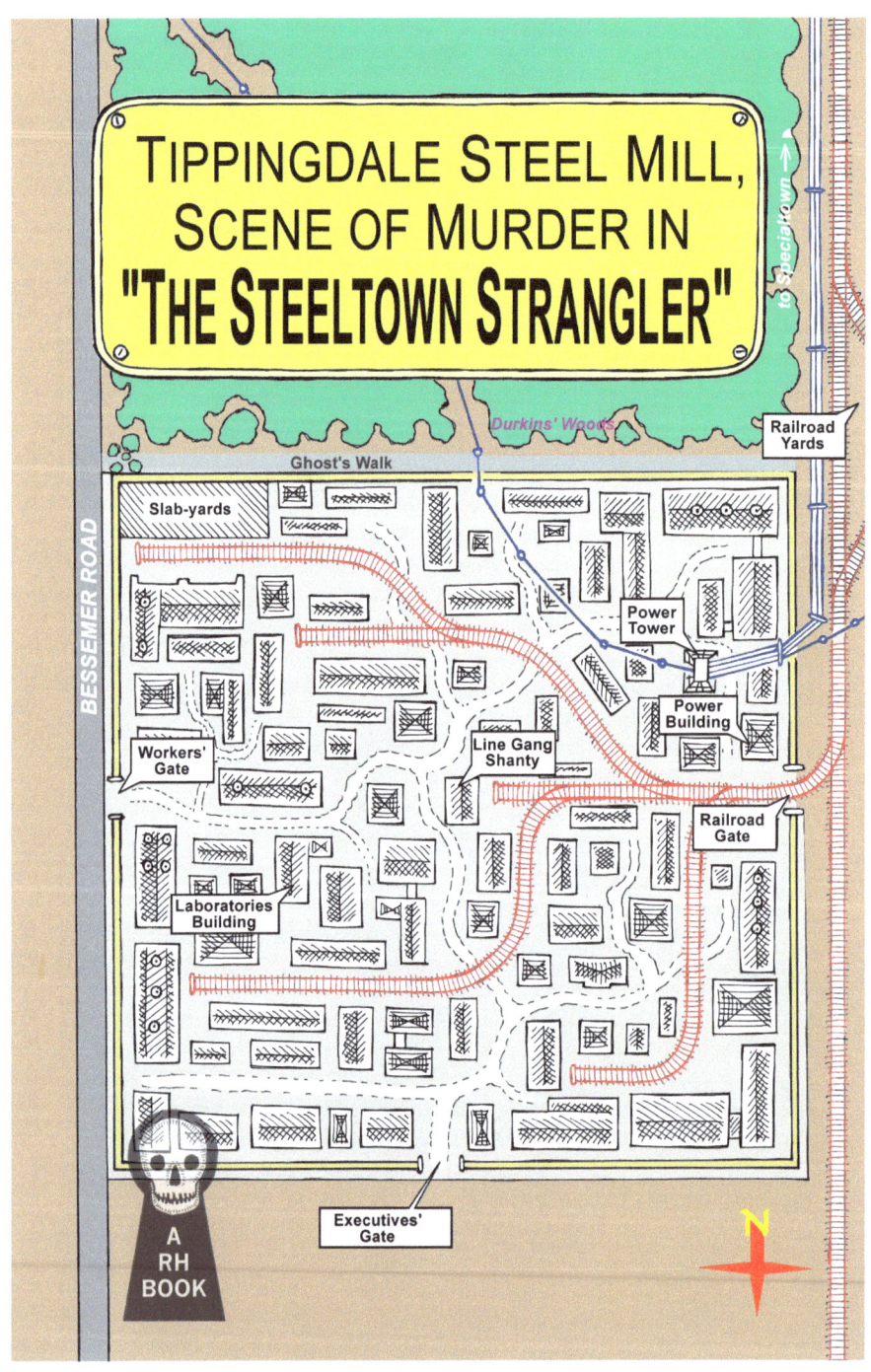

The Steeltown Strangler (1950)

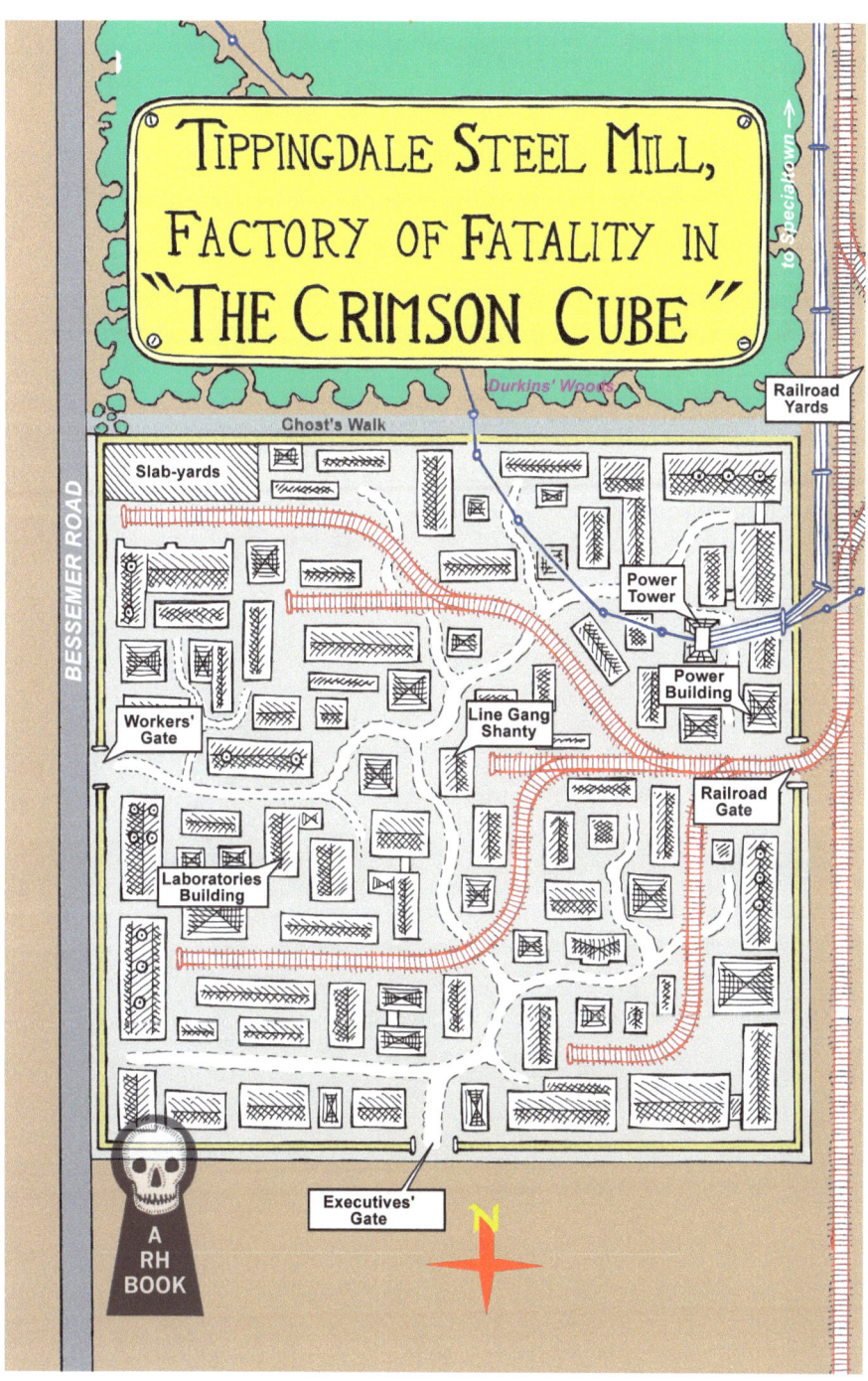

The Crimson Cube (1954)

The Trap

As opposed to Keeler's tendency to fashion 'alternate-reality' cities for some of his novels, in *The Trap* he places most of the characters and pivotal plot events in a *real* town, namely Comanche, Oklahoma. Curiously, *Keeler's* town of Comanche, Oklahoma, seems to bear little resemblance to its real-life counterpart!

Current residents of Comanche, Oklahoma, beware: please do *not* use this map to navigate your way around town! I suspect that Comanche-ites will never run the risk of driving down Speckled Hen Road nor of fishing from the banks of the Pinto River.[1] Suffice to say I based my map design purely on Keeler's story, and was unable to make any use whatsoever of modern maps of the 'real' Comanche.

This novel was published here for the first time, making it a mapback first edition.

---

1. If any person at the moment resident in Comanche, Oklahoma, lives in Lame Goose Road, please let us know!

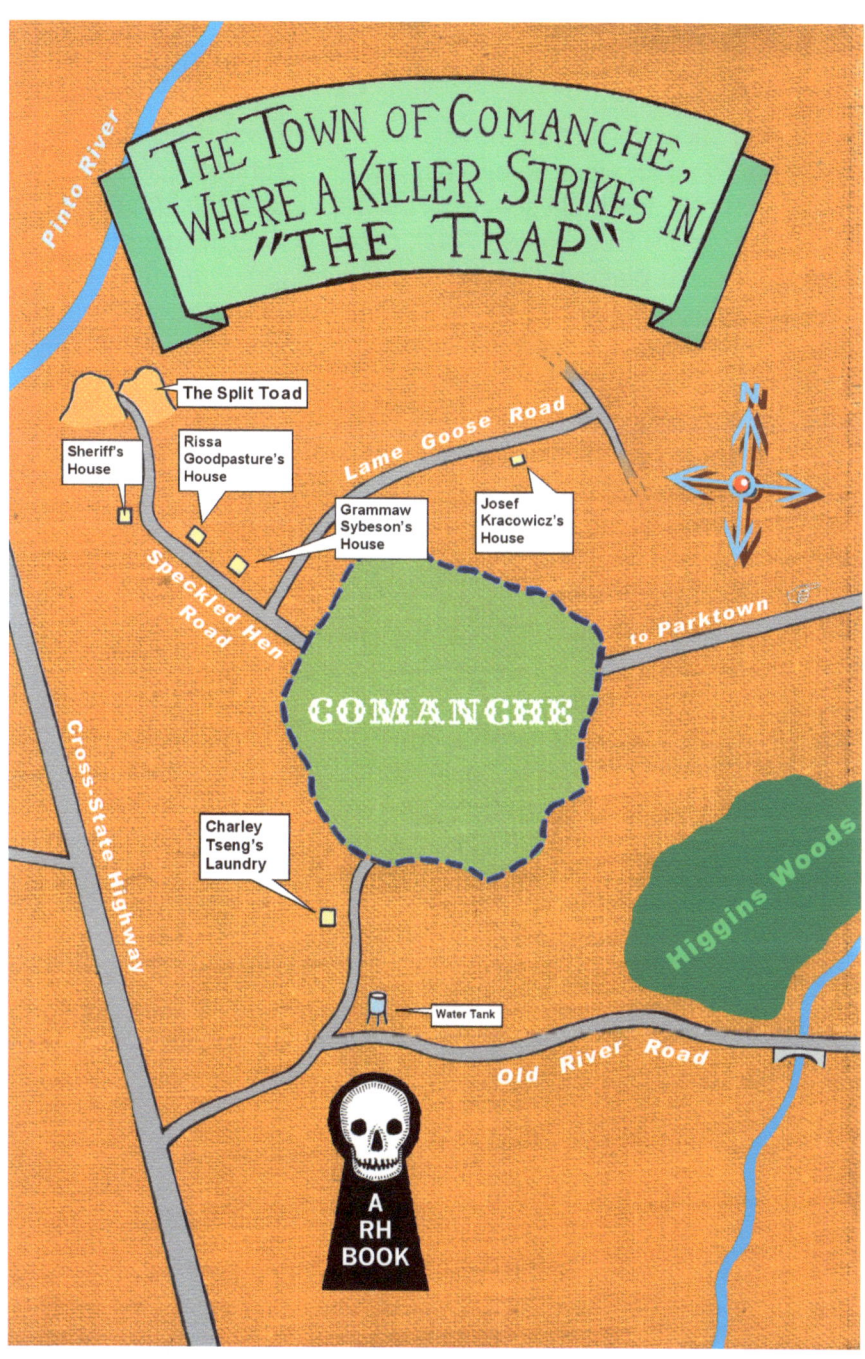

The Trap
(1956)

The White Circle & *Strange Journey*

These epic 'skience friction' novels, co-written with Keeler's second wife Tertza Rinaldo, were among the author's last books. As in *I Killed Lincoln at 10:13!*, the main scene is Ramble House, the large rooming-house on Cotton Tree Road, Washington D.C. The events of *The White Circle* take place in the 1950s and *Strange Journey* in 1967.[1]

Relatively unchanged on the outside, and still a rooming-house, Ramble House has followed the fashions in interior design during the hundred years since the assassination of Abraham Lincoln. With one exception: the large room previously occupied by Phineas Steerforth which has since become leased to Professor Tiberius Heatherwick, a "temporarily expatriated Britisher." Heatherwick has substantially altered the layout of the room to introduce a bit of 'nature' for his peace-of-mind: the room now has a green carpet, a park bench and artificial squirrel to simulate the beloved parks of his memory. As well as this, a large white circle has been painted on the green carpet (as previously found in *The White Circle*). Since the Professor's untimely death, his will has stipulated the room remain exactly as it is. Those wishing to discover the purpose of this circle are invited to read the book.

The description of the room in this book and *The White Circle* is so detailed that I found it fairly straightforward delineating it. I was further assisted by making reference to Richard Polt's earlier design showing the layout of the room. [2]

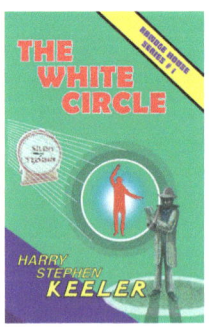 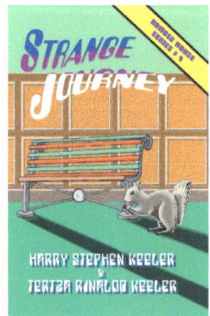

1. For a comprehensive and detailed account of Keeler's *Ramble House* series novels, see Fender Tucker's *The House of Ramble* introduction to *I Killed Lincoln at 10:13!* and *Strange Journey* (both published by Ramble House, 2004).

2. Previously published in *Keeler News* and the introduction to *The White Circle*.

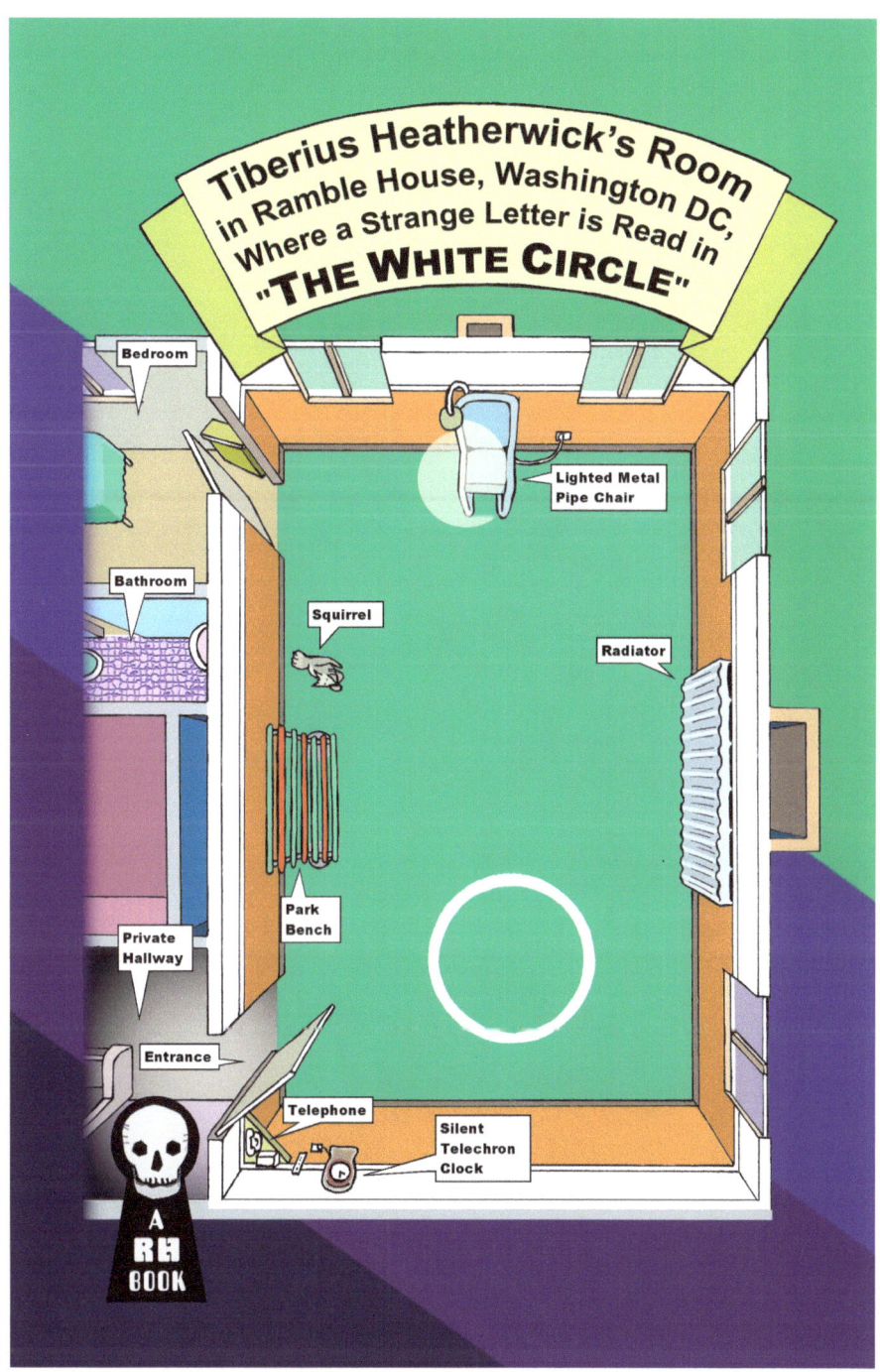

The White Circle (1965)

Strange Journey (1965)

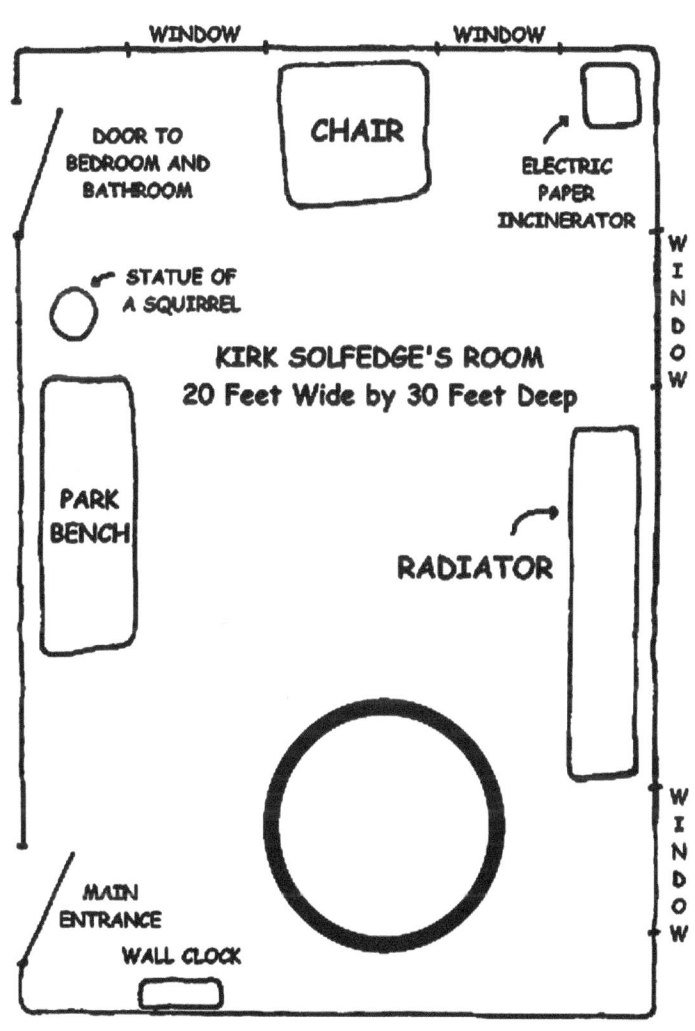

Hand-drawn Map of the Room
from The House of Ramble

I Killed Lincoln At 10:13!

Ramble House,[1] the large rooming-house originally built and owned by Horace Tarwater and situated on Cotton Tree Road, Washington D.C., appears in five books: *The White Circle*, the present novel, *The Sign of the Crossed Leaves*, *The Purple Room* and *The Strange Journey* (termed the 'Ramble House series'). Each book is set in different time periods (and within several novels, within several time periods during the story) and the house is described consistently by Keeler, hence my relative ease at portraying the building.[2]

This book is set during the events of April 14, 1865, when American President Abraham Lincoln was assassinated at Ford's Theater, Washington D.C. by John Wilkes Booth. This epic novel is steeped in the fervor and tragedy of the assassination and the American Civil War conflict.

Again a straightforward rendering of the house, with subtle inclusion of the Confederate flag in the title banner, and scanned woodgrain as a background.

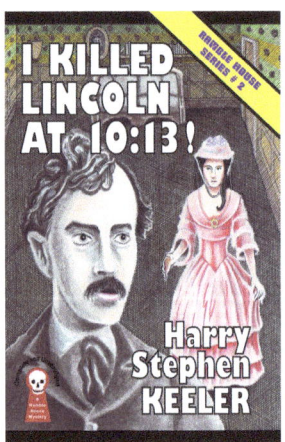

---

1. It is from this building that the current esteemed publisher has adopted its name.

2. Artist's note: Despite Keeler's good description of Ramble House, my depiction of the building may not be entirely true to the scale and minute detail as originally envisaged by the author. Readers may rest assured, however, that the basic layout and juxtaposition of rooms are accurate, and should provide a helpful guide to putting the events of the book into some visual perspective.

I Killed Lincoln at 10:13! (1958)

The Straw Hat Murders

This previously unpublished late Keeler novel is also one of his shorter mysteries. As with details of scenes and buildings in many of Keeler's novels, the description of the Goldfarb building at 633 South Street is well-rounded. This, together with the relatively simple layout of the building, made devising a diagram of the building and its neighbors, with pertinent cut-outs to show interior details, nice and straightforward.

The Straw Hat Murders (1958)

The Affair of the Bottled Deuce

The Affair of the Bottled Deuce is a nicely-constructed locked-room death mystery which takes place in Mr. Marchesi's rather run-down apartment building in Chicago's 'Little Italy.' To my knowledge, Leaf and Pelligrini Streets (on the intersection of which the apartment building is situated) are fictitious creations of Keeler's.

As in previous Keeler mapback designs, I've echoed the look and layout of the traditional Dell mapbacks. The massive, windowless warehouse looms large behind the flats, a silent and blind backdrop to the furtive activities of the protagonists. The rear ground level courtyard of the Marchesi flats could only be shown by cutting away part of the actual building.

Lythgoe Crockett's room and the Marchesi flats are fairly well described in this novel. However, there were several aspects of the layout of the building which were only vaguely described, so I have tried to fill in those details within the general layout as apparent in the text.

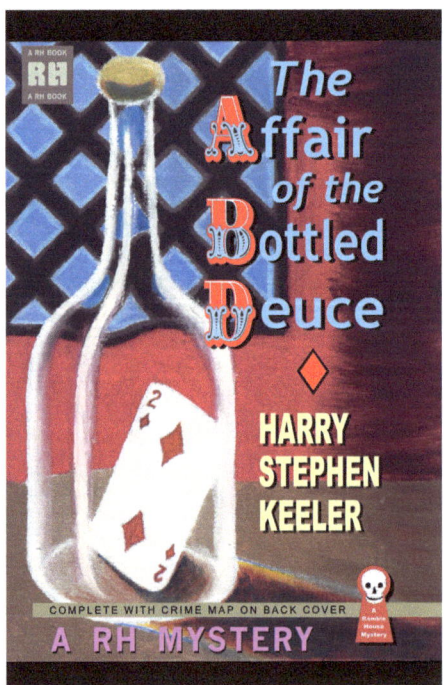

The Affair of the Bottled Deuce (1958)

The Footprints of Satan

In his 1950 novel *The Footprints of Satan* Norman Berrow incorporates the legend of The Devon Devil into a masterful and atmospheric crime thriller.

In 1855, in Southern Devon, a series of footprints were found in new morning snow, meandering around a village, and even traversing rooftops; rumour quickly spread that only the Devil himself could have been responsible. In Berrow's adaptation, no less a meandering trail is discovered by townsfolk of Steeple Thelming, though this time more than rumour is at issue—there is a murder involved.[1]

The trail of footprints in the snow, at first so mysterious and 'impossible,' prove to be comparable to a 'locked-room' scenario, and it remains for sleuthing minds to work out the logical unravelling of physical possibilities and whereabouts of the prime suspects.

Most of Berrow's crime novels involve the strong suggestion of supernatural forces at play within a murder case, and this book is an excellent example of the balance of commonsense police-work challenging and dispelling superstition.

1. A similar 'snowy' scenario is involved in Hake Talbot's *The Rim of the Pit*, a classic crime novel reprinted by Ramble House, using an adaptation of its original mapback cover.

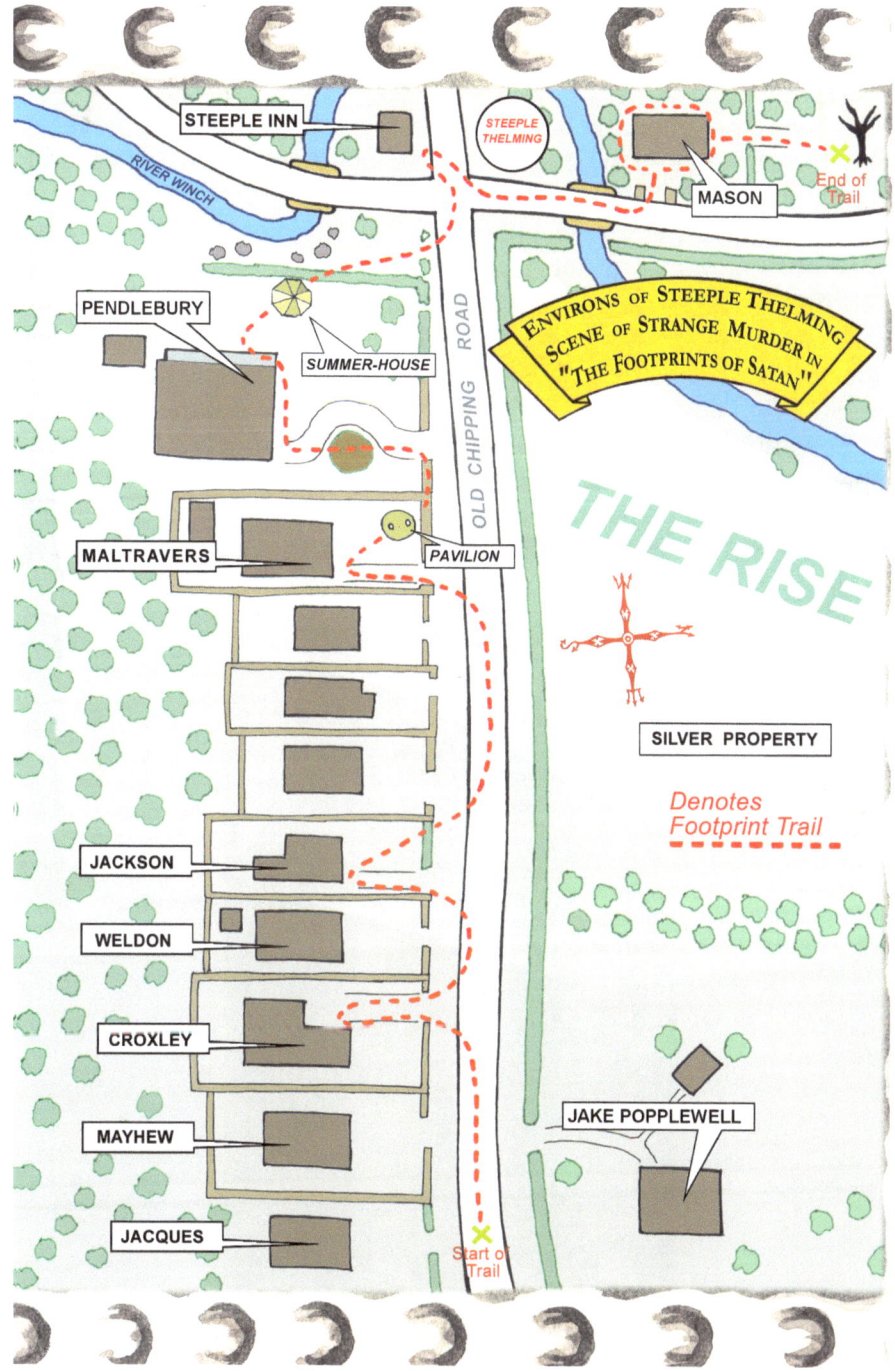

The Footprints of Satan
by Norman Berrow (1950)

Marblehead

2006 saw the publication by Ramble House of this epic novel as originally envisaged by Lupoff (an abridged, rewritten version had been published in 1985 as *Lovecraft's Book.*[1])

I referenced various historical sites on the internet to capture the geographical details of the town of Marblehead, MA, c.1927. I also had the benefit of being able to call on the author for advice about certain specific details— a great assistance for the mapback-maker (most of my latter-day mapback-creation has been assisted by ever-helpful living authors).

Several islands and such-like in Marblehead Harbor and Marblehead Channel currently own different names than they did in 1927, but concerted searches through old naval charts, generously made available on the internet, helped resolve these sites for the mapback.

---

1. See Fender Tucker's introduction to *Marblehead* for the history of this novel.

Marblehead
by Richard A. Lupoff (2006)

The Universal Holmes

This masterful collection of short stories, inspired by the character and world of the great Sherlock Holmes, contains a tale which also draws in elements derived from the supernatural world of H. P. Lovecraft.

In 'The Adventure of the Voorish Sign,' the feverish and dramatic events culminate in a visit to a most amazing black structure in the Arctic wastes: the Anthracite Palace. In this mapback, I have attempted to give a basic delineation of a grand building which is almost as convoluted an edifice as Gormenghast.[1]

Again, I was helped by the author in arriving at this treatment of the cut-away building; Richard Lupoff kindly supplied examples of similar cut-away treatments of old castles.

---

1. Gormenghast is the all-encompassing and age-old castle central to English author Mervyn Peake's novels *Titus Groan* (1946) and *Gormenghast* (1950).

The Universal Holmes
by Richard A. Lupoff (2007)

The Secret Adventures of Sherlock Holmes

As with Dick Lupoff's collection of Sherlock Holmes tales, Gary Lovisi was an indispensable help in providing reference material and copies of old maps of London to assist me in coming up with this contemporary map of London, pertinent to the events in Gary's story 'The Adventure of the Missing Detective.'

The task is so much easier for me when I can seek advice about specific geography from the author himself; the authors have already researched histories and locales during their writing, and such authority makes my job a relatively straightforward one.

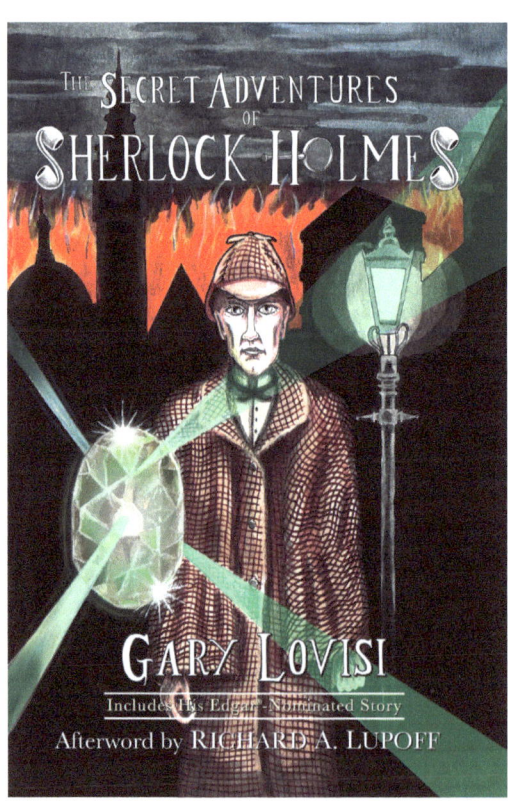

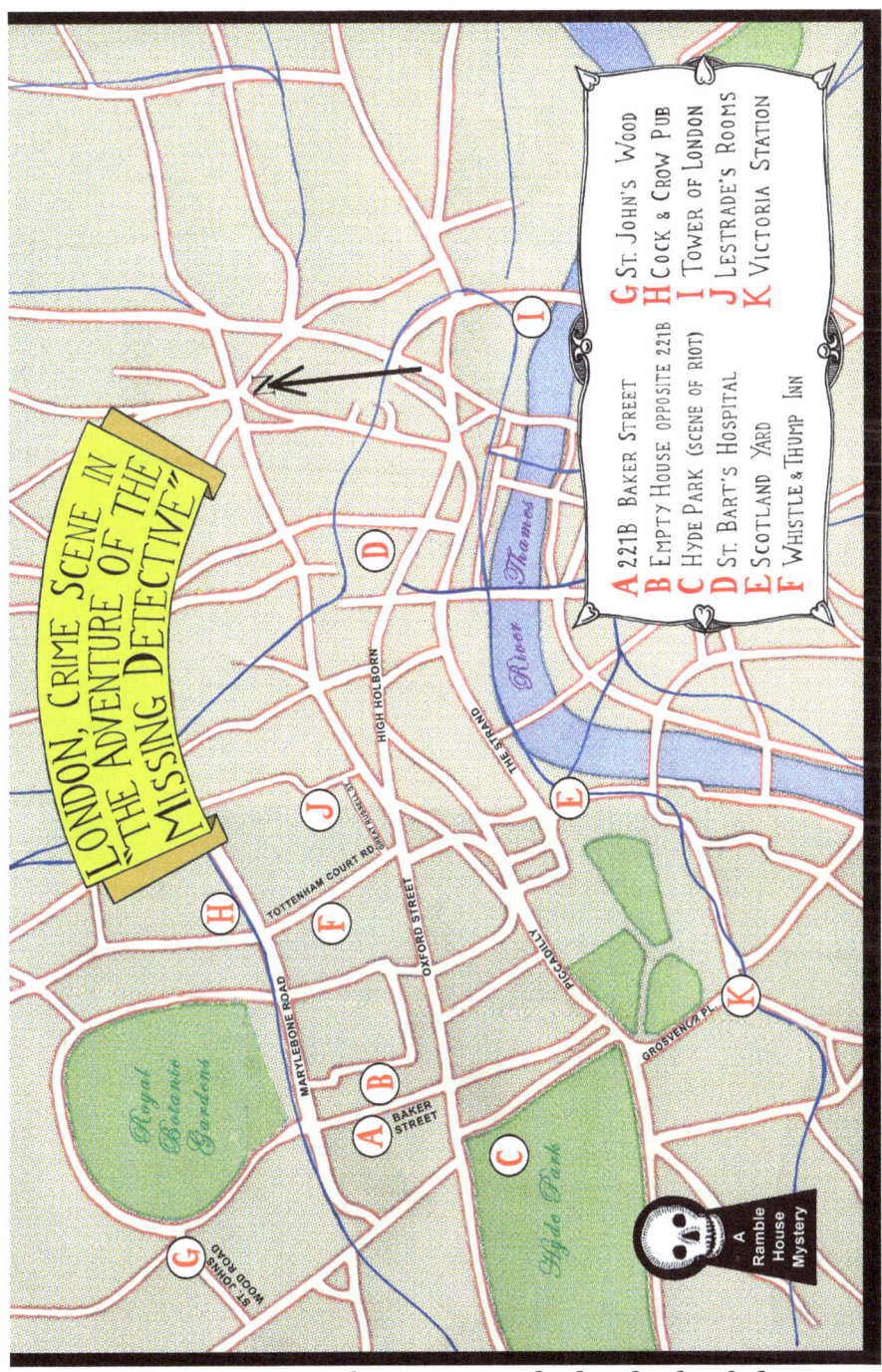

London, Crime Scene in "The Adventure of the Missing Detective"

A 221B Baker Street
B Empty House opposite 221B
C Hyde Park (scene of riot)
D St. Bart's Hospital
E Scotland Yard
F Whistle & Thump Inn
G St. John's Wood
H Cock & Crow Pub
I Tower of London
J Lestrade's Rooms
K Victoria Station

The Secret Adventures of Sherlock Holmes
by Gary Lovisi (2007)

The Naked Trocar

Fender's dark tale of nefarious goings-on in and around Farmington, NM, was even more geographically-informed than the previous books — Fender himself is an ex-Farmington resident, and he knows the district well enough to give very precise details about the area. This made my work on this mapback a real pleasure.

Fender and I did need to work out the best way to present the classic 'large' and 'small' views of Farmington, as various events take place outside the city limits. What, on the face of it, can seem like a simple presentation of two views becomes slightly more complex when you have to account for certain sites in one map but not the other, whilst keeping both clear and easy to read.

There's nothing worse than a map that is impossible to understand. As an accompaniment to a story, it's crucial that the map be a benefit rather than an impediment.

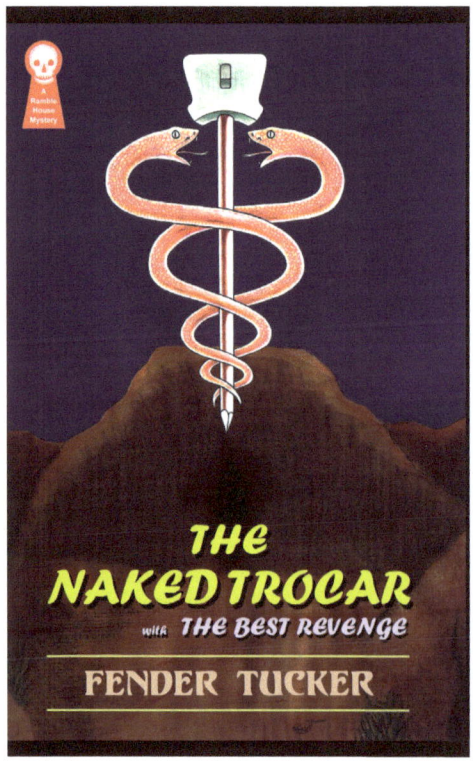

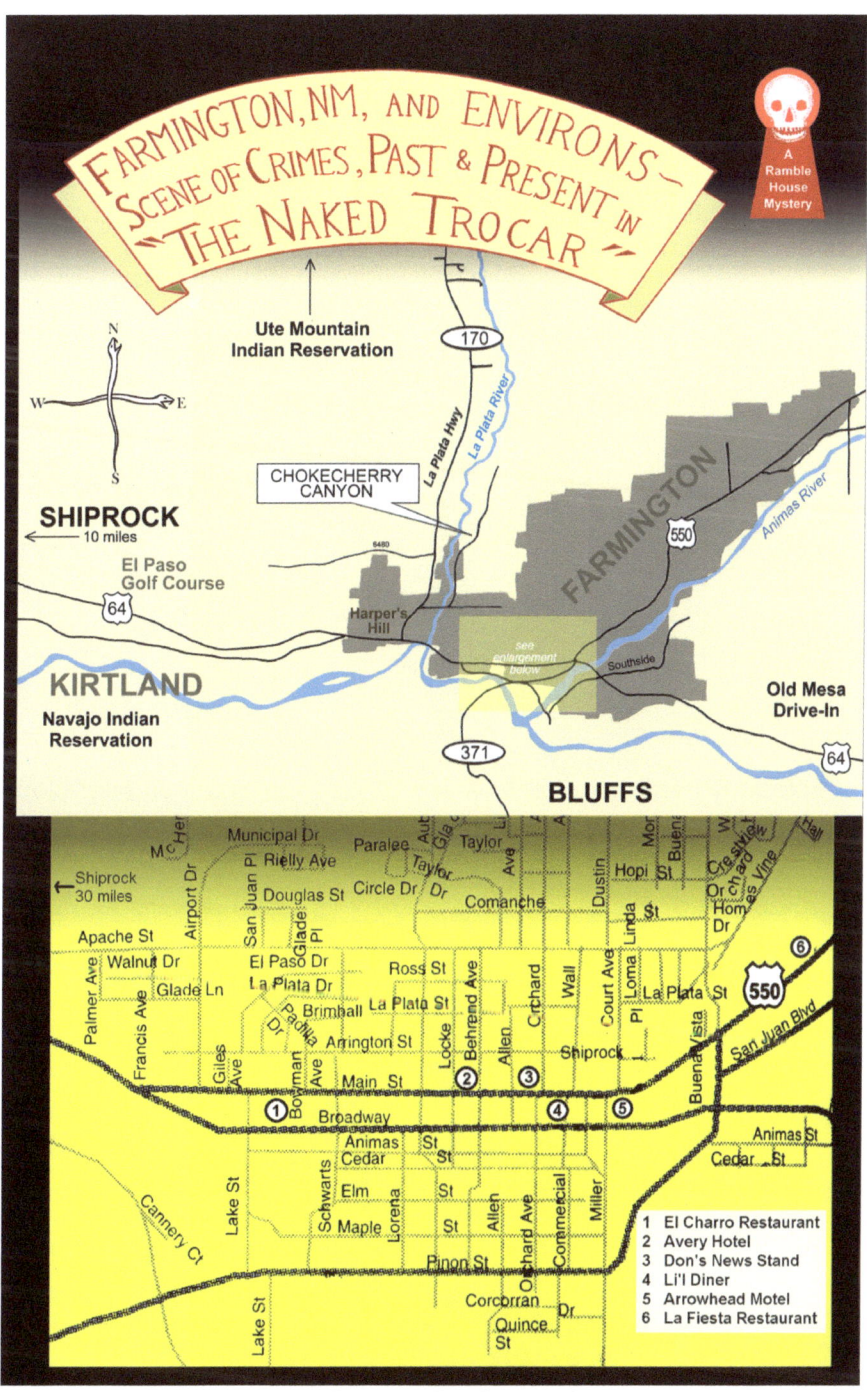

The Naked Trocar
by Fender Tucker (2007)

Fatal Accident

I was greatly assisted in my creation of this mapback, not by the living author, but by a "sketch plan of accident" scene as provided by the policeman Glaves in the novel; this plan is reproduced on the endpapers of the original British edition of the book *(as below)*:

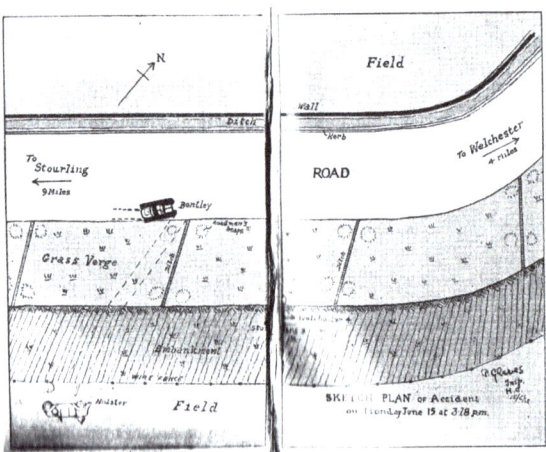

I adapted my mapback from this sketch plan, turning it counter-clockwise to place it more conveniently (and more northerly) on the book's cover. I redrew all the elements, tinted certain areas in basic colour, and generally cleaned the plan up.

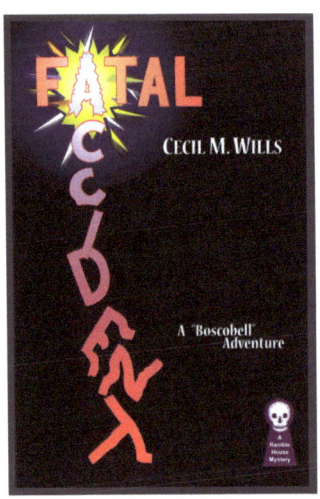

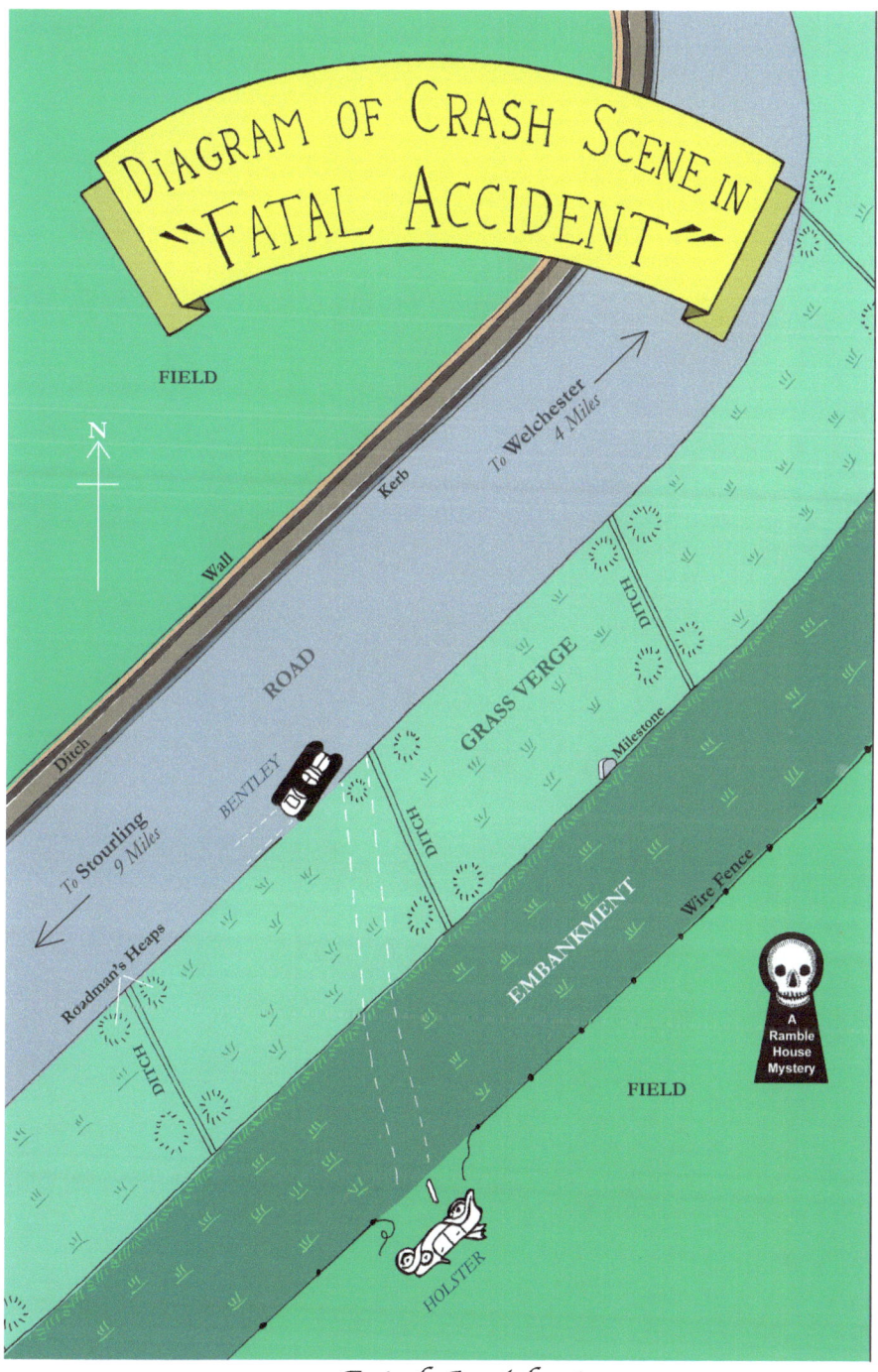

Fatal Accident
by Cecil M. Wills (1936)

The Finger of Destiny and Other Stories

This collection of haunting stories by Edmund Snell is #42 in the Dancing Tuatara Press imprint sequence. These stories are set on the island of Borneo, and the mapback shows Borneo and surrounding islands.

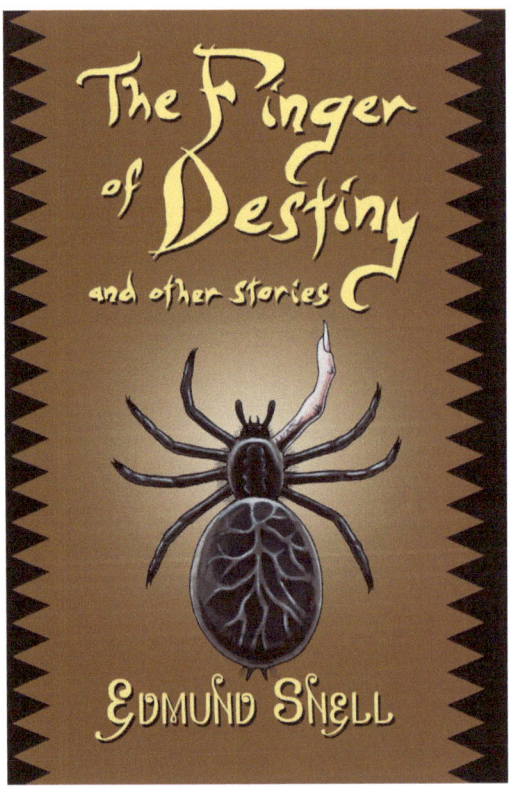

The Finger of Destiny and Other Stories
Edmund Snell (1938)

Murder Among the Nudists

Peter Hunt's murder mystery set in a nudist camp was first published in 1934, and was the last in the Alan Miller series of mystery novels. This mapback depicts a bird's eye view of the nudist camp. The front cover was a design incorporating a 'magic eye' 3D image.

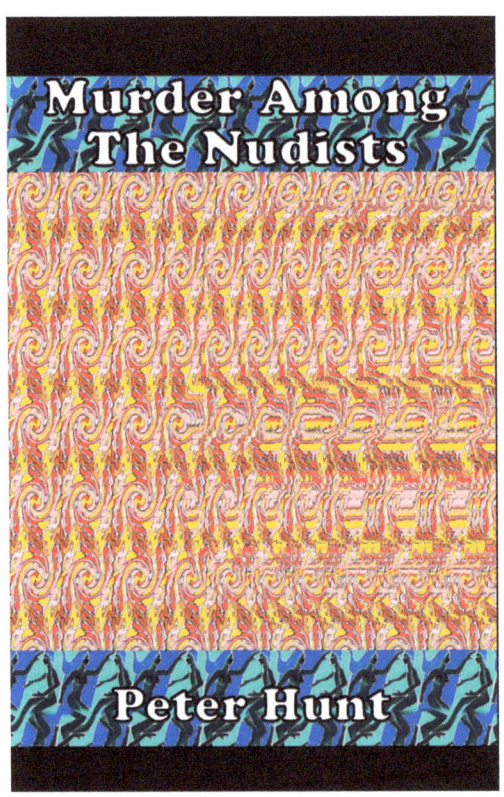

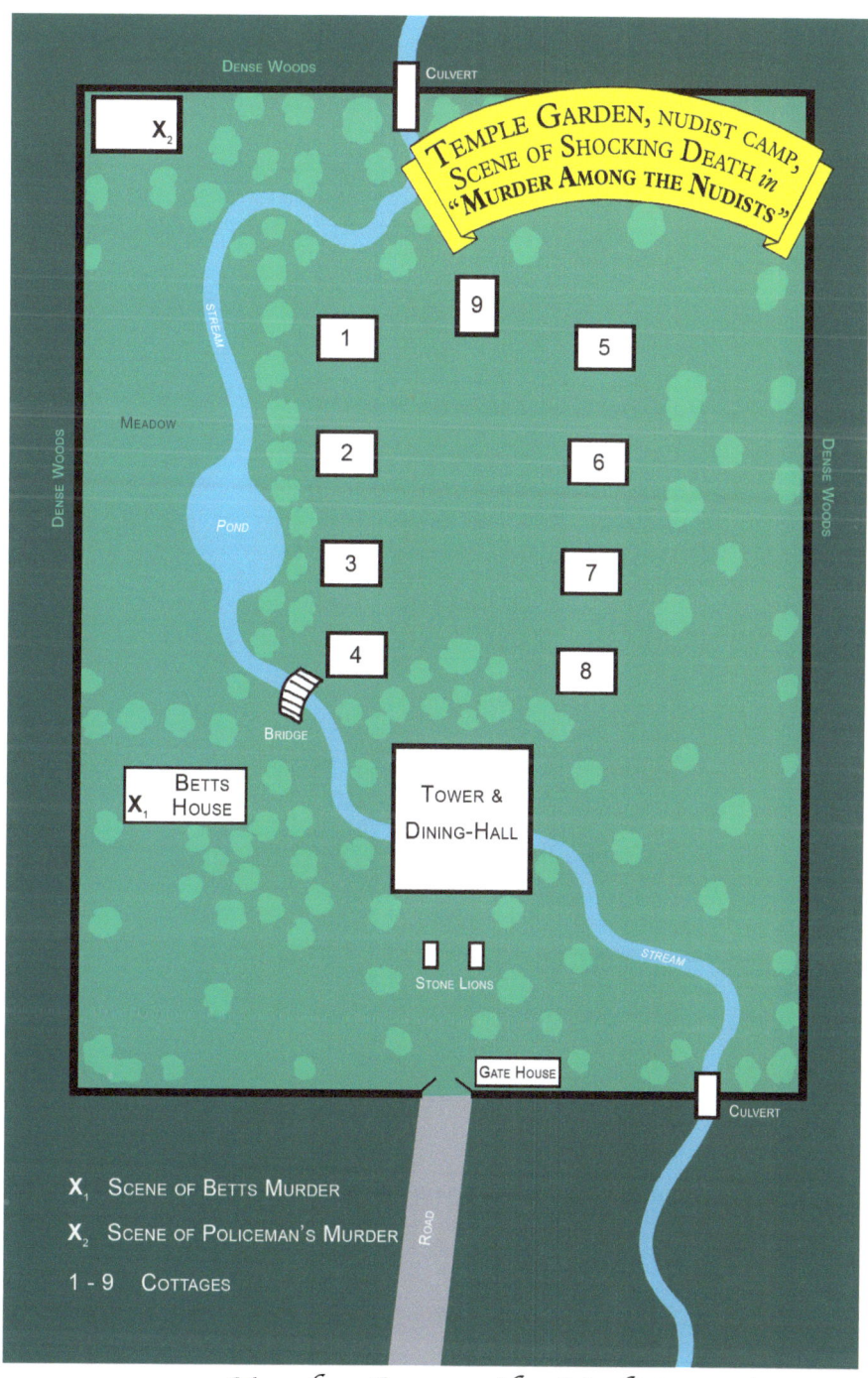

DENSE WOODS   CULVERT

X₂

TEMPLE GARDEN, NUDIST CAMP,
SCENE OF SHOCKING DEATH *in*
"MURDER AMONG THE NUDISTS"

STREAM

9

1   5

MEADOW

2   6

POND

3   7

4   8

BRIDGE

BETTS
X₁ HOUSE

TOWER &
DINING-HALL

STREAM

STONE LIONS

GATE HOUSE

CULVERT

DENSE WOODS

X₁ SCENE OF BETTS MURDER

X₂ SCENE OF POLICEMAN'S MURDER

ROAD

1 - 9 COTTAGES

Murder Among the Nudists
by Peter Hunt (1934)

The Picaroons

This novel by American authors Gelett Burgess and Will Irwin is set in San Francisco in 1904 (two years before that city would suffer a devastating earthquake). The mapback for the book is based on contemporary references; I was also much assisted by the book's editor and introducer, Richard A. Lupoff. This book is #6 in the Surinam Turtle Press imprint sequence.

The Picaroons
by Gelett Burgess & Will Irwin (1904)

Win, Place and Die!

This novel by American writer Milton K. Ozaki (1913-1989) is an original publication, having remained unpublished at the time of the author's death. The mapback design is based on the author's own sketch of the casino layout, with the addition of a few glitzy graphics suggestive of a modern gambling house. This book is #39 in the Surinam Turtle Press imprint sequence.

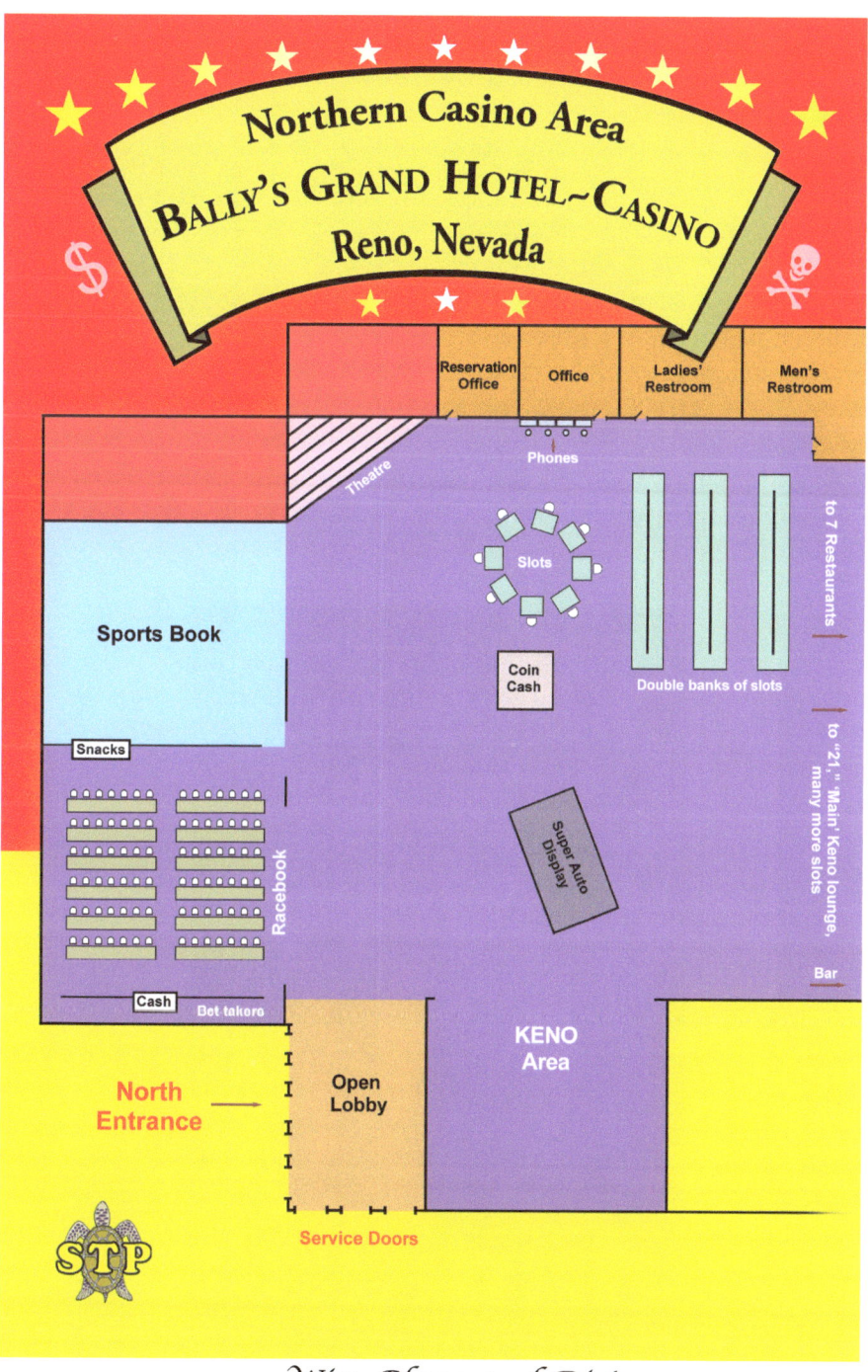

Win, Place and Die!
by Milton K. Ozaki (2013)

The Baddington Horror

When Fender Tucker suggested that this novel by Walter S. Masterman cried out for a mapback, I jumped at the chance to design a map for its back cover. As I've done several times before, I set to reading the book with the design of the mansion central to the story, Baddington Court, uppermost in my mind. I pieced together the author's references to the details of the house, and managed to arrive at a fairly good approximation of the house layout. As it happened, we decided to focus on the area surrounding the murder scene, and this part of the house and grounds were well-described regularly through the story, making it a straightforward task to contrive a clear map of the Secret Garden and environs.

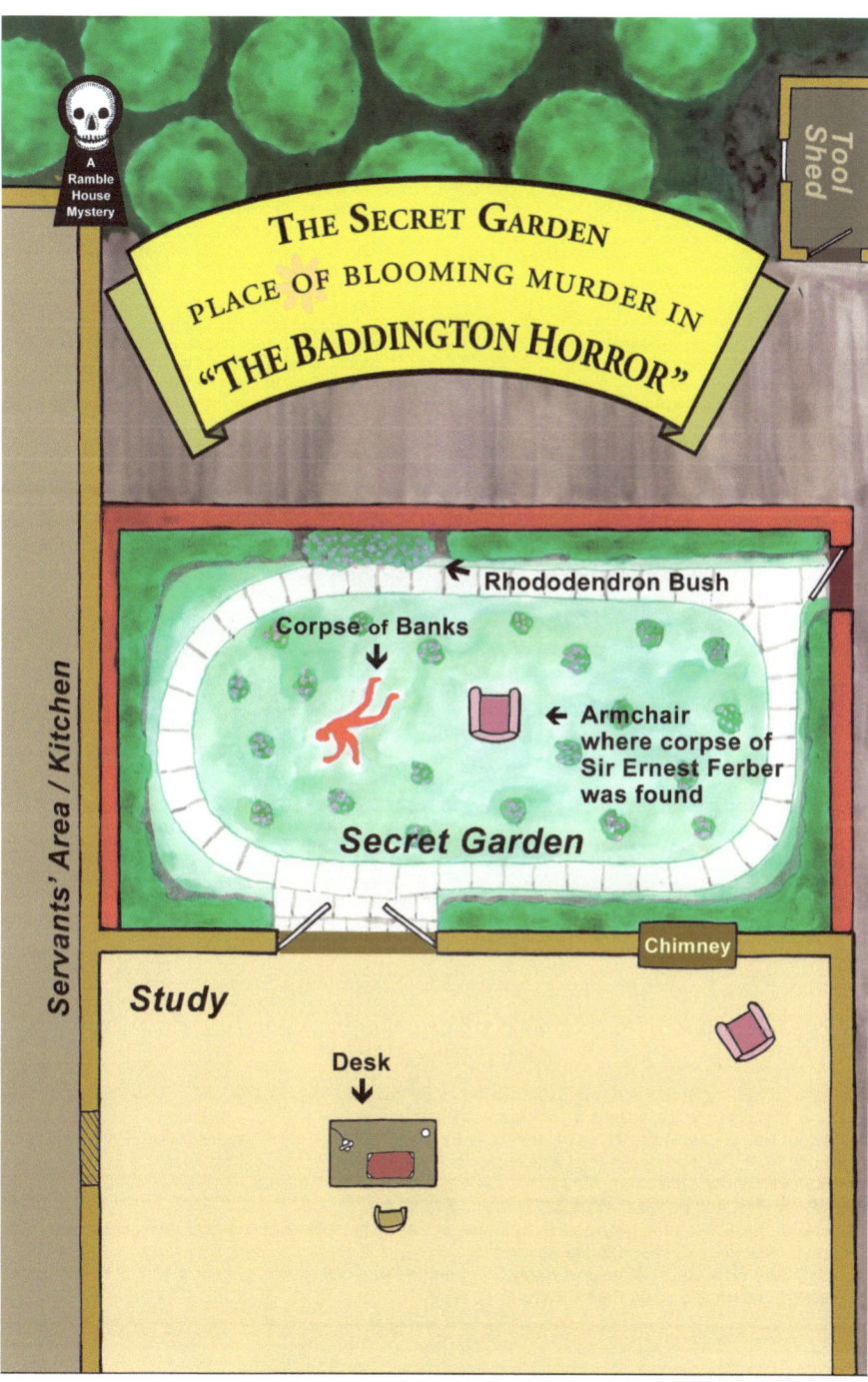

The Baddington Horror
by Walter S. Masterman (1934)

RAMBLE HOUSE's

HARRY STEPHEN KEELER WEBWORK MYSTERIES

(RH) indicates the title is available ONLY in the RAMBLE HOUSE edition

The Ace of Spades Murder
The Affair of the Bottled Deuce (RH)
The Amazing Web
The Barking Clock
Behind That Mask
The Book with the Orange Leaves
The Bottle with the Green Wax Seal
The Box from Japan
The Case of the Canny Killer
The Case of the Crazy Corpse (RH)
The Case of the Flying Hands (RH)
The Case of the Ivory Arrow
The Case of the Jeweled Ragpicker
The Case of the Lavender Gripsack
The Case of the Mysterious Moll
The Case of the 16 Beans
The Case of the Transparent Nude (RH)
The Case of the Transposed Legs
The Case of the Two-Headed Idiot (RH)
The Case of the Two Strange Ladies
The Circus Stealers (RH)
Cleopatra's Tears
A Copy of Beowulf (RH)
The Crimson Cube (RH)
The Face of the Man From Saturn
Find the Clock
The Five Silver Buddhas
The 4th King
The Gallows Waits, My Lord! (RH)
The Green Jade Hand
Finger! Finger!
Hangman's Nights (RH)
I, Chameleon (RH)
I Killed Lincoln at 10:13! (RH)
The Iron Ring
The Man Who Changed His Skin (RH)
The Man with the Crimson Box
The Man with the Magic Eardrums
The Man with the Wooden Spectacles
The Marceau Case
The Matilda Hunter Murder

The Monocled Monster
The Murder of London Lew
The Murdered Mathematician
The Mysterious Card (RH)
The Mysterious Ivory Ball of Wong Shing Li (RH)
The Mystery of the Fiddling Cracksman
The Peacock Fan
The Photo of Lady X (RH)
The Portrait of Jirjohn Cobb
Report on Vanessa Hewstone (RH)
Riddle of the Travelling Skull
Riddle of the Wooden Parrakeet (RH)
The Scarlet Mummy (RH)
The Search for X-Y-Z
The Sharkskin Book
Sing Sing Nights
The Six From Nowhere (RH)
The Skull of the Waltzing Clown
The Spectacles of Mr. Cagliostro
Stand By—London Calling!
The Steeltown Strangler
The Stolen Gravestone (RH)
Strange Journey (RH)
The Strange Will
The Straw Hat Murders (RH)
The Street of 1000 Eyes (RH)
Thieves' Nights
Three Novellos (RH)
The Tiger Snake
The Trap (RH)
Vagabond Nights (Defrauded Yeggman)
Vagabond Nights 2 (10 Hours)
The Vanishing Gold Truck
The Voice of the Seven Sparrows
The Washington Square Enigma
When Thief Meets Thief
The White Circle (RH)
The Wonderful Scheme of Mr. Christopher Thorne
X. Jones—of Scotland Yard
Y. Cheung, Business Detective

Keeler Related Works

A To Izzard: A Harry Stephen Keeler Companion by Fender Tucker — Articles and stories about Harry, by Harry, and in his style. Included is a compleat bibliography.

Wild About Harry: Reviews of Keeler Novels — Edited by Richard Polt & Fender Tucker — 22 reviews of works by Harry Stephen Keeler from *Keeler News*. A perfect introduction to the author.

The Keeler Keyhole Collection: Annotated newsletter rants from Harry Stephen Keeler, edited by Francis M. Nevins. Over 400 pages of incredibly personal Keeleriana.

Fakealoo — Pastiches of the style of Harry Stephen Keeler by selected demented members of the HSK Society. Updated every year with the new winner.

Strands of the Web: Short Stories of Harry Stephen Keeler — 29 stories, just about all that Keeler wrote, are edited and introduced by Fred Cleaver.

RAMBLE HOUSE's Loon Sanctuary

A Clear Path to Cross — Sharon Knowles short mystery stories by Ed Lynskey.

A Jimmy Starr Omnibus — Three 40s novels by Jimmy Starr.

A Niche in Time and Other Stories — Classic SF by William F. Temple

A Roland Daniel Double: The Signal and The Return of Wu Fang — Classic thrillers from the 30s.

A Shot Rang Out — Three decades of reviews and articles by today's Anthony Boucher, Jon Breen. An essential book for any mystery lover's library.

A Smell of Smoke — A 1951 English countryside thriller by Miles Burton.

A Snark Selection — Lewis Carroll's *The Hunting of the Snark* with two Snarkian chapters by Harry Stephen Keeler — Illustrated by Gavin L. O'Keefe.

A Young Man's Heart — A forgotten early classic by Cornell Woolrich.

Alexander Laing Novels — *The Motives of Nicholas Holtz* and *Dr. Scarlett*, stories of medical mayhem and intrigue from the 30s.

An Angel in the Street — Modern hardboiled noir by Peter Genovese.

Automaton — Brilliant treatise on robotics: 1928-style! By H. Stafford Hatfield.

Away From the Here and Now — Clare Winger Harris stories, collected by Richard A. Lupoff

Beast or Man? — A 1930 novel of racism and horror by Sean M'Guire. Introduced by John Pelan.

Black Hogan Strikes Again — Australia's Peter Renwick pens a tale of the 30s outback.

Black River Falls — Suspense from the master, Ed Gorman.

Blondy's Boy Friend — A snappy 1930 story by Philip Wylie, writing as Leatrice Homesley.

Blood in a Snap — The *Finnegan's Wake* of the 21st century, by Jim Weiler.

Blood Moon — The first of the Robert Payne series by Ed Gorman.

Bogart '48 — Hollywood action with Bogie by John Stanley and Kenn Davis

Calling Lou Largo! — Two Lou Largo novels by William Ard.

Cornucopia of Crime — Francis M. Nevins assembled this huge collection of his writings about crime literature and the people who write it. Essential for any serious mystery library.

Corpse Without Flesh — Strange novel of forensics by George Bruce.

Crimson Clown Novels — By Johnston McCulley, author of the Zorro novels, *The Crimson Clown* and *The Crimson Clown Again.*

Dago Red — 22 tales of dark suspense by Bill Pronzini.

Dark Sanctuary — Weird Menace story by H. B. Gregory

David Hume Novels — *Corpses Never Argue, Cemetery First Stop, Make Way for the Mourners, Eternity Here I Come.* 1930s British hardboiled fiction with an attitude.

Dead Man Talks Too Much — Hollywood boozer by Weed Dickenson.

Death Leaves No Card — One of the most unusual murdered-in-the-tub mysteries you'll ever read. By Miles Burton.

Death March of the Dancing Dolls and Other Stories — Volume Three in the Day Keene in the Detective Pulps series. Introduced by Bill Crider.

Deep Space and other Stories — A collection of SF gems by Richard A. Lupoff.

Detective Duff Unravels It — Episodic mysteries by Harvey O'Higgins.

Diabolic Candelabra — Classic 30s mystery by E.R. Punshon

Dime Novels: Ramble House's 10-Cent Books — *Knife in the Dark* by Robert Leslie Bellem, *Hot Lead* and *Song of Death* by Ed Earl Repp, *A Hashish House in New York* by H.H. Kane, and five more.

Don Diablo: Book of a Lost Film — Two-volume treatment of a western by Paul Landres, with diagrams. Intro by Francis M. Nevins.

Dope and Swastikas — Two strange novels from 1922 by Edmund Snell

Dope Tales #1 — Two dope-riddled classics; *Dope Runners* by Gerald Grantham and *Death Takes the Joystick* by Phillip Condé.

Dope Tales #2 — Two more narco-classics; *The Invisible Hand* by Rex Dark and *The Smokers of Hashish* by Norman Berrow.

Dope Tales #3 — Two enchanting novels of opium by the master, Sax Rohmer. *Dope* and *The Yellow Claw.*

Double Hot — Two 60s softcore sex novels by Morris Hershman.

Dr. Odin — Douglas Newton's 1933 racial potboiler comes back to life.

Evangelical Cockroach — Jack Woodford writes about writing.

Evidence in Blue — 1938 mystery by E. Charles Vivian.

Fatal Accident — Murder by automobile, a 1936 mystery by Cecil M. Wills.

Fighting Mad — Todd Robbins' 1922 novel about boxing and life

Finger-prints Never Lie — A 1939 classic detective novel by John G. Brandon.

Freaks and Fantasies — Eerie tales by Tod Robbins, collaborator of Tod Browning on the film FREAKS.

Gadsby — A lipogram (a novel without the letter E). Ernest Vincent Wright's last work, published in 1939 right before his death.

Gelett Burgess Novels — *The Master of Mysteries, The White Cat, Two O'Clock Courage, Ladies in Boxes, Find the Woman, The Heart Line, The Picaroons* and *Lady Mechante*. Recently added is A Gelett Burgess Sampler, edited by Alfred Jan. All are introduced by Richard A. Lupoff.

Geronimo — S. M. Barrett's 1905 autobiography of a noble American.

Hake Talbot Novels — *Rim of the Pit, The Hangman's Handyman.* Classic locked room mysteries, with mapback covers by Gavin O'Keefe.

Hands Out of Hell and Other Stories — John H. Knox's eerie hallucinations

Hell is a City — William Ard's masterpiece.

Hollywood Dreams — A novel of Tinsel Town and the Depression by Richard O'Brien.

Hostesses in Hell and Other Stories — Russell Gray's most graphic stories

House of the Restless Dead — Strange and ominous tales by Hugh B. Cave

I Stole $16,000,000 — A true story by cracksman Herbert E. Wilson.

Inclination to Murder — 1966 thriller by New Zealand's Harriet Hunter.

Invaders from the Dark — Classic werewolf tale from Greye La Spina.

J. Poindexter, Colored — Classic satirical black novel by Irvin S. Cobb.

Jack Mann Novels — Strange murder in the English countryside. *Gees' First Case, Nightmare Farm, Grey Shapes, The Ninth Life, The Glass Too Many, Her Ways Are Death, The Kleinert Case* and *Maker of Shadows.*

Jake Hardy — A lusty western tale from Wesley Tallant.

Jim Harmon Double Novels — *Vixen Hollow/Celluloid Scandal, The Man Who Made Maniacs/Silent Siren, Ape Rape/Wanton Witch, Sex Burns Like Fire/Twist Session, Sudden Lust/Passion Strip, Sin Unlimited/Harlot Master, Twilight Girls/Sex Institution.* Written in the early 60s and never reprinted until now.

Joel Townsley Rogers Novels and Short Stories — By the author of *The Red Right Hand: Once In a Red Moon, Lady With the Dice, The Stopped Clock, Never Leave My Bed.* Also two short story collections: *Night of Horror* and *Killing Time.*

John Carstairs, Space Detective — Arboreal Sci-fi by Frank Belknap Long

Joseph Shallit Novels — *The Case of the Billion Dollar Body, Lady Don't Die on My Doorstep, Kiss the Killer, Yell Bloody Murder, Take Your Last Look.* One of America's best 50's authors and a favorite of author Bill Pronzini.

Keller Memento — 45 short stories of the amazing and weird by Dr. David Keller.

Killer's Caress — Cary Moran's 1936 hardboiled thriller.

Lady of the Yellow Death and Other Stories — More stories by Wyatt Blassingame.

League of the Grateful Dead and Other Stories — Volume One in the Day Keene in the Detective Pulps series.

Library of Death — Ghastly tale by Ronald S. L. Harding, introduced by John Pelan

Malcolm Jameson Novels and Short Stories — *Astonishing! Astounding!, Tarnished Bomb, The Alien Envoy and Other Stories* and *The Chariots of San Fernando and Other Stories.* All introduced and edited by John Pelan or Richard A. Lupoff.

Man Out of Hell and Other Stories — Volume II of the John H. Knox weird pulps collection.

Marblehead: A Novel of H.P. Lovecraft — A long-lost masterpiece from Richard A. Lupoff. This is the "director's cut", the long version that has never been published before.

Master of Souls — Mark Hansom's 1937 shocker is introduced by weirdologist John Pelan.

Max Afford Novels — *Owl of Darkness, Death's Mannikins, Blood on His Hands, The Dead Are Blind, The Sheep and the Wolves, Sinners in Paradise* and *Two Locked Room Mysteries and a Ripping Yarn* by one of Australia's finest mystery novelists.

Money Brawl — Two books about the writing business by Jack Woodford and H. Bedford-Jones. Introduced by Richard A. Lupoff.

More Secret Adventures of Sherlock Holmes — Gary Lovisi's second collection of tales about the unknown sides of the great detective.

Muddled Mind: Complete Works of Ed Wood, Jr. — David Hayes and Hayden Davis deconstruct the life and works of the mad, but canny, genius.

Murder among the Nudists — A mystery from 1934 by Peter Hunt, featuring a naked Detective-Inspector going undercover in a nudist colony.

Murder in Black and White — 1931 classic tennis whodunit by Evelyn Elder.

Murder in Shawnee — Two novels of the Alleghenies by John Douglas: *Shawnee Alley Fire* and *Haunts*.

Murder in Silk — A 1937 Yellow Peril novel of the silk trade by Ralph Trevor.

My Deadly Angel — 1955 Cold War drama by John Chelton.

My First Time: The One Experience You Never Forget — Michael Birchwood — 64 true first-person narratives of how they lost it.

Mysterious Martin, the Master of Murder — Two versions of a strange 1912 novel by Tod Robbins about a man who writes books that can kill.

Norman Berrow Novels — *The Bishop's Sword, Ghost House, Don't Go Out After Dark, Claws of the Cougar, The Smokers of Hashish, The Secret Dancer, Don't Jump Mr. Boland!, The Footprints of Satan, Fingers for Ransom, The Three Tiers of Fantasy, The Spaniard's Thumb, The Eleventh Plague, Words Have Wings, One Thrilling Night, The Lady's in Danger, It Howls at Night, The Terror in the Fog, Oil Under the Window, Murder in the Melody, The Singing Room.* This is the complete Norman Berrow library of locked-room mysteries, several of which are masterpieces.

Old Faithful and Other Stories — SF classic tales by Raymond Z. Gallun

Old Times' Sake — Short stories by James Reasoner from Mike Shayne Magazine.

One Dreadful Night — A classic mystery by Ronald S. L. Harding

Pair O' Jacks — A mystery novel and a diatribe about publishing by Jack Woodford

Perfect .38 — Two early Timothy Dane novels by William Ard. More to come.

Prince Pax — Devilish intrigue by George Sylvester Viereck and Philip Eldridge

Prose Bowl — Futuristic satire of a world where hack writing has replaced football as our national obsession, by Bill Pronzini and Barry N. Malzberg.

Red Light — The history of legal prostitution in Shreveport Louisiana by Eric Brock. Includes wonderful photos of the houses and the ladies.

Researching American-Made Toy Soldiers — A 276-page collection of a lifetime of articles by toy soldier expert Richard O'Brien.

Reunion in Hell — Volume One of the John H. Knox series of weird stories from the pulps. Introduced by horror expert John Pelan.

Ripped from the Headlines! — The Jack the Ripper story as told in the newspaper articles in the *New York* and *London Times*.

Robert Randisi Novels — *No Exit to Brooklyn* and *The Dead of Brooklyn*. The first two Nick Delvecchio novels.

Rough Cut & New, Improved Murder — Ed Gorman's first two novels.

R.R. Ryan Novels — Freak Museum and The Subjugated Beast, two horror classics.

Ruled By Radio — 1925 futuristic novel by Robert L. Hadfield & Frank E. Farncombe.

Rupert Penny Novels — *Policeman's Holiday, Policeman's Evidence, Lucky Policeman, Policeman in Armour, Sealed Room Murder, Sweet Poison, The Talkative Policeman, She had to Have Gas* and *Cut and Run* (by Martin Tanner.) Rupert Penny is the pseudonym of Australian Charles Thornett, a master of the locked room, impossible crime plot.

Sacred Locomotive Flies — Richard A. Lupoff's psychedelic SF story.

Sam — Early gay novel by Lonnie Coleman.

Sand's Game — Spectacular hard-boiled noir from Ennis Willie, edited by Lynn Myers and Stephen Mertz, with contributions from Max Allan Collins, Bill Crider, Wayne Dundee, Bill Pronzini, Gary Lovisi and James Reasoner.

Sand's War — More violent fiction from the typewriter of Ennis Willie

Satan's Den Exposed — True crime in Truth or Consequences New Mexico — Award-winning journalism by the *Desert Journal*.

Satans of Saturn — Novellas from the pulps by Otis Adelbert Kline and E. H. Price

Satan's Sin House and Other Stories — Horrific gore by Wayne Rogers

Secrets of a Teenage Superhero — Graphic lit by Jonathan Sweet

Sex Slave — Potboiler of lust in the days of Cleopatra by Dion Leclerq, 1966.

Shadows' Edge — Two early novels by Wade Wright: *Shadows Don't Bleed* and *The Sharp Edge*.

Sideslip — 1968 SF masterpiece by Ted White and Dave Van Arnam.

Slammer Days — Two full-length prison memoirs: *Men into Beasts* (1952) by George Sylvester Viereck and *Home Away From Home* (1962) by Jack Woodford.

Slippery Staircase — 1930s whodunit from E.C.R. Lorac

Sorcerer's Chessmen — John Pelan introduces this 1939 classic by Mark Hansom.

Star Griffin — Michael Kurland's 1987 masterpiece of SF drollery is back.

Stakeout on Millennium Drive — Award-winning Indianapolis Noir by Ian Woollen.

Strands of the Web: Short Stories of Harry Stephen Keeler — Edited and Introduced by Fred Cleaver.

Summer Camp for Corpses and Other Stories — Weird Menace tales from Arthur Leo Zagat; introduced by John Pelan.

Suzy — A collection of comic strips by Richard O'Brien and Bob Vojtko from 1970.

Tales of the Macabre and Ordinary — Modern twisted horror by Chris Mikul, author of the *Bizarrism* series.

Tenebrae — Ernest G. Henham's 1898 horror tale brought back.

The Alice Books — Lewis Carroll wrote them; Gavin L. O'Keefe illustrated them

The Amorous Intrigues & Adventures of Aaron Burr — by Anonymous. Hot historical action about the man who almost became Emperor of Mexico.

The Anthony Boucher Chronicles — edited by Francis M. Nevins. Book reviews by Anthony Boucher written for the *San Francisco Chronicle,* 1942 – 1947. Essential and fascinating reading by the best book reviewer there ever was.

The Barclay Catalogs — Two essential books about toy soldier collecting by Richard O'Brien

The Basil Wells Omnibus — A collection of Wells' stories by Richard A. Lupoff.

The Beautiful Dead and Other Stories — Dreadful tales from Donald Dale

The Best of 10-Story Book — edited by Chris Mikul, over 35 stories from the literary magazine Harry Stephen Keeler edited.

The Black Dark Murders — Vintage 50s college murder yarn by Milt Ozaki, writing as Robert O. Saber.

The Book of Time — The classic novel by H.G. Wells is joined by sequels by Wells himself and three stories by Richard A. Lupoff. Illustrated by Gavin L. O'Keefe.

The Case in the Clinic — One of E.C.R. Lorac's finest.

The Case of the Bearded Bride — #4 in the Day Keene in the Detective Pulps series

The Case of the Little Green Men — Mack Reynolds wrote this love song to sci-fi fans back in 1951 and it's now back in print.

The Case of the Withered Hand — 1936 potboiler by John G. Brandon.

The Charlie Chaplin Murder Mystery — A 2004 tribute by noted film scholar, Wes D. Gehring.

The Compleat Calhoon — All of Fender Tucker's works: Includes *Totah Six-Pack, Weed, Women and Song* and *Tales from the Tower,* plus a CD of all of his songs.

The Compleat Ova Hamlet — Parodies of SF authors by Richard A. Lupoff. This is a brand new edition with more stories and more illustrations by Trina Robbins.

The Contested Earth and Other SF Stories — A never-before published space opera and seven short stories by Jim Harmon.

The Crimson Query — A 1929 thriller from Arlton Eadie. A perfect way to get introduced.

The Curse of Cantire — Classic 1939 novel of a family curse by Walter S. Masterman.

The Devil and the C.I.D. — Odd diabolic mystery by E.C.R. Lorac

The Devil Drives — An odd prison and lost treasure novel from 1932 by Virgil Markham.

The Devil's Mistress — A 1915 Scottish gothic tale by J. W. Brodie-Innes, a member of Aleister Crowley's Golden Dawn.

The Devil's Nightclub and Other Stories — John Pelan introduces some gruesome tales by Nat Schachner.

The Disentanglers — Episodic intrigue at the turn of last century by Andrew Lang

The Dumpling — Political murder from 1907 by Coulson Kernahan.

The End of It All and Other Stories — Ed Gorman selected his favorite short stories for this huge collection.

The Fangs of Suet Pudding — A 1944 novel of the German invasion by Adams Farr

The Ghost of Gaston Revere — From 1935, a novel of life and beyond by Mark Hansom, introduced by John Pelan.

The Girl in the Dark — A thriller from Roland Daniel

The Gold Star Line — Seaboard adventure from L.T. Reade and Robert Eustace.

The Golden Dagger — 1951 Scotland Yard yarn by E. R. Punshon.

The Great Orme Terror — Horror stories by Garnett Radcliffe from the pulps

The Hairbreadth Escapes of Major Mendax — Francis Blake Crofton's 1889 boys' book.

The House That Time Forgot and Other Stories — Insane pulpitude by Robert F. Young

The House of the Vampire — 1907 poetic thriller by George S. Viereck.

The Illustrious Corpse — Murder hijinx from Tiffany Thayer

The Incredible Adventures of Rowland Hern — Intriguing 1928 impossible crimes by Nicholas Olde.

The Julius Caesar Murder Case — A classic 1935 re-telling of the assassination by Wallace Irwin that's much more fun than the Shakespeare version.

The Koky Comics — A collection of all of the 1978-1981 Sunday and daily comic strips by Richard O'Brien and Mort Gerberg, in two volumes.

The Lady of the Terraces — 1925 missing race adventure by E. Charles Vivian.

The Lord of Terror — 1925 mystery with master-criminal, Fantômas.

The Melamare Mystery — A classic 1929 Arsene Lupin mystery by Maurice Leblanc

The Man Who Was Secrett — Epic SF stories from John Brunner

The Man Without a Planet — Science fiction tales by Richard Wilson

The N. R. De Mexico Novels — Robert Bragg, the real N.R. de Mexico, presents *Marijuana Girl, Madman on a Drum, Private Chauffeur* in one volume.

The Night Remembers — A 1991 Jack Walsh mystery from Ed Gorman.

The One After Snelling — Kickass modern noir from Richard O'Brien.

The Organ Reader — A huge compilation of just about everything published in the 1971-1972 radical bay-area newspaper, *THE ORGAN*. A coffee table book that points out the shallowness of the coffee table mindset.

The Poker Club — Three in one! Ed Gorman's ground-breaking novel, the short story it was based upon, and the screenplay of the film made from it.

The Private Journal & Diary of John H. Surratt — The memoirs of the man who conspired to assassinate President Lincoln.

The Secret Adventures of Sherlock Holmes — Three Sherlockian pastiches by the Brooklyn author/publisher, Gary Lovisi.

The Shadow on the House — Mark Hansom's 1934 masterpiece of horror is introduced by John Pelan.

The Sign of the Scorpion — A 1935 Edmund Snell tale of oriental evil.

The Singular Problem of the Stygian House-Boat — Two classic tales by John Kendrick Bangs about the denizens of Hades.

The Smiling Corpse — Philip Wylie and Bernard Bergman's odd 1935 novel.

The Spider: Satan's Murder Machines — A thesis about Iron Man.

The Stench of Death: An Odoriferous Omnibus by Jack Moskovitz — Two complete novels and two novellas from 60's sleaze author, Jack Moskovitz.

The Story Writer and Other Stories — Classic SF from Richard Wilson

The Strange Case of the Antlered Man — 1935 dementia from Edwy Searles Brooks

The Strange Thirteen — Richard B. Gamon's odd stories about Raj India.

The Technique of the Mystery Story — Carolyn Wells' tips about writing.

The Threat of Nostalgia — A collection of his most obscure stories by Jon Breen

The Time Armada — Fox B. Holden's 1953 SF gem.

The Tongueless Horror and Other Stories — Volume One of the series of short stories from the weird pulps by Wyatt Blassingame.

The Tracer of Lost Persons — From 1906, an episodic novel that became a hit radio series in the 30s. Introduced by Richard A. Lupoff.

The Trail of the Cloven Hoof — Diabolical horror from 1935 by Arlton Eadie. Introduced by John Pelan.

The Triune Man — Mindscrambling science fiction from Richard A. Lupoff.

The Unholy Goddess and Other Stories — Wyatt Blassingame's first DTP compilation

The Universal Holmes — Richard A. Lupoff's 2007 collection of five Holmesian pastiches and a recipe for giant rat stew.

The Werewolf vs the Vampire Woman — Hard to believe ultraviolence by either Arthur M. Scarm or Arthur M. Scram.

The Whistling Ancestors — A 1936 classic of weirdness by Richard E. Goddard and introduced by John Pelan.

The White Owl — A vintage thriller from Edmund Snell

The White Peril in the Far East — Sidney Lewis Gulick's 1905 indictment of the West and assurance that Japan would never attack the U.S.

The Wizard of Berner's Abbey — A 1935 horror gem written by Mark Hansom and introduced by John Pelan.

The Wonderful Wizard of Oz — by L. Frank Baum and illustrated by Gavin L. O'Keefe

Time Line — Ramble House artist Gavin O'Keefe selects his most evocative art inspired by the twisted literature he reads and designs.

Tiresias — Psychotic modern horror novel by Jonathan M. Sweet.

Totah Six-Pack — Fender Tucker's six tales about Farmington in one sleek volume.

Trail of the Spirit Warrior — Roger Haley's historical saga of life in the Indian Territories.

Two Kinds of Bad — Two 50s novels by William Ard about Danny Fontaine

Two Suns of Morcali and Other Stories — Evelyn E. Smith's SF tour-de-force

Ultra-Boiled — 23 gut-wrenching tales by our Man in Brooklyn, Gary Lovisi.

Up Front From Behind — A 2011 satire of Wall Street by James B. Kobak.

Victims & Villains — Intriguing Sherlockiana from Derham Groves.

Wade Wright Novels — *Echo of Fear, Death At Nostalgia Street, It Leads to Murder* and *Shadows' Edge*, a double book featuring *Shadows Don't Bleed* and *The Sharp Edge.*

Walter S. Masterman Novels — *The Green Toad, The Flying Beast, The Yellow Mistletoe, The Wrong Verdict, The Perjured Alibi, The Border Line, The Bloodhounds Bay* and *The Curse of Cantire.* Masterman wrote horror and mystery, some introduced by John Pelan.

We Are the Dead and Other Stories — Volume Two in the Day Keene in the Detective Pulps series, introduced by Ed Gorman. When done, there may be as many as 11 in the series.

Welsh Rarebit Tales — Charming stories from 1902 by Harle Oren Cummins

West Texas War and Other Western Stories — by Gary Lovisi.

Whip Dodge: Man Hunter — Wesley Tallant's saga of a bounty hunter of the old West.

Win, Place and Die! — The first new mystery by Milt Ozaki in decades. The ultimate novel of 70s Reno.

You'll Die Laughing — Bruce Elliott's 1945 novel of murder at a practical joker's English countryside manor.

RAMBLE HOUSE

Fender Tucker, Prop.   Gavin L. O'Keefe, Graphics

www.ramblehouse.com   fender@ramblehouse.com

228-826-1783   10329 Sheephead Drive, Vancleave MS 39565

www.ingramcontent.com/pod-product-compliance
Lightning Source LLC
Chambersburg PA
CBHW042004050726
47507CB00025B/69